Thicker
Than
Water

Other

Father Dowling Mysteries

HER DEATH OF COLD

THE SEVENTH STATION

BISHOP AS PAWN

LYING THREE

SECOND VESPERS

Also by

Ralph McInerny

QUICK AS A DODO

THICKER THAN WATER

by

Ralph McInerny

FATHER DOWLING
Mystery

THE VANGUARD PRESS
NEW YORK

Published by Vanguard Press, Inc., 424 Madison Avenue, New York, N.Y. 10017. Published simultaneously in Canada by Beatty & Church, Toronto, Ontario. All rights reserved.

Library of Congress Cataloging in Publication Data

McInerny, Ralph M.
   Thicker than water.

   I. Title.
PS3563.A31166T47   1981   813′.54   81–10432
ISBN 0–8149–0858–6   AACR2

Designer: Tom Torre Bevans

Manufactured in the United States of America.

2 3 4 5 6 7 8 9 0

For Tom Stritch

Thicker Than Water

1

THAT FEBRUARY afternoon at the St. Hilary rectory in Fox River, Illinois, several things happened that made Mrs. Murkin, the housekeeper, something less than the cheerful self she had resolved to be, no matter that six gloomy weeks of Lent stretched ahead of her. Several things happened, no one of them terribly important in itself, but when she considered them all together, she didn't like it one bit.

First, there was the matter of the offering box in the rear of the church. There was nothing new in the fact that parishioners, or whoever, in search of spiritual reading had a way of paying a good deal less than face value for the literature they took. The prices were clearly marked on the covers of the magazines and pamphlets—for a time Marie Murkin had encircled the prices with a red felt-tip pen until Father Dowling told her to stop it—but somehow there was always a discrepancy between the value of the reading matter taken and the money Mrs. Murkin found in the offering box.

"I'm glad enough that they take the stuff," Father Dowling told her. "The parish can afford to subsidize Lenten reading."

"It isn't just during Lent."

"Marie, it really doesn't matter."

"Stealing doesn't matter?"

He frowned at her. If Father Dowling were put in charge of the Last Judgment, there wouldn't be many who didn't make it through the Pearly Gates. He reminded her of the sign over the magazine rack. HELP YOURSELF. "If you like, we can describe it as free literature, Marie."

"This time it's different."

"How so?"

"It's not just that they're not putting enough in. Someone's been taking money out."

It was true. Someone had jimmied the slot of the money box and fished out all but a few coins. For twenty-five dollars' worth of pamphlets and magazines, St. Hilary's parish had received seventeen cents. Father Dowling went over to the church with her and looked sadly at the damaged money box. Right then and there he lettered the sign. FREE LITERATURE.

"Have Feeney remove the box, Marie."

"That's your solution?"

That was his solution. It was all Marie could do not to telephone Captain Keegan and let him know what was going on at St. Hilary's. What stopped her was imagining Phil Keegan's reaction. He would call it a crime wave and make her feel silly. But Captain Keegan would not have dismissed the second episode.

At two in the afternoon, Marie Murkin liked to slip up to her room and lie down on the bed. To rest. She drew a blanket over her and she held a crystal rosary in her hand as if what she meant to do was pray, but invariably within a minute or two she was asleep. She would sleep for half an hour, almost exactly, scarcely a minute either way, before waking up refreshed and ready for the remaining chores of her day. The main task was the preparation of the evening meal. And that was the second thing.

When she came down her back staircase into the kitchen the chops she had been defrosting were no longer on the drain board of the sink.

At first she thought she was losing her mind. She had a distinct memory of putting the meat there, yet it was not there. Could she possibly have imagined doing that? She went down to the basement to the freezer, wondering if she would be able to tell from its contents whether or not she had already taken out chops. But before she opened the door of the freezer her attention was captured by the empty shelves beside it. Her jams and jellies were gone! Her cry was as much one of surprise as of dismay.

"When were you last down there?" Father Dowling asked. At least he wasn't laughing this away. How could he? Those jams and jellies represented hours of work, let alone the cost of the fruit and sugar and jars and the rest.

"I took out the chops while you were eating lunch."

"Twelve-thirty, a little later?"

"Yes. And I'm sure the jars were there then. I would have noticed. It happened after two."

"How do you know?"

"The pork chops are gone from the kitchen. They were there when I went up to my room at two."

"You didn't hear a thing?"

"No. They must have taken the jams and jellies and the pork chops too."

"They?"

"Whoever it was."

Father Dowling looked at his watch. It was not yet three. "I was saying my office."

After the pastor inspected the empty shelves, they returned to the study. Father Dowling sat at his desk and deliberately filled a pipe with tobacco. Watching the lean priest devote his whole attention to that task, Marie Murkin tried not to lose her temper.

"Should I call Captain Keegan?"

You would have thought she had told a joke. "No, Marie. I don't think so."

"Father Dowling, a theft has occurred here. A second theft. You can smile if you want to, but this is a crime wave. First the money from the church, now all the preserves from the cellar. Plus four pork chops." She paused as if to let him imagine what might not be taken next if they did not act quickly.

"Was the door locked?"

"It wasn't forced. You saw that."

"I didn't really notice."

"They tracked up my kitchen floor."

Father Dowling shook his head in wonderment. "I didn't hear a thing."

Marie Murkin just looked at him. Whenever Father Dowling was reading his office, he tuned out the whole world. You could light a fire under his chair or drop a firecracker in the room and he would go on mumbling over his breviary. Not that she was criticizing. That's what a priest is for, praying, and a person should do well what he is supposed to do. But even so, how on earth could he just sit here while strangers strolled into the house and walked brazenly off with their winter's supply of preserves?

"How many trips would it take, Marie?"

She thought about that. It was a good question. Last fall Feeney had helped her take the jars of jams and jellies down to the basement. Feeney wasn't much help but even so she calculated it would take one person at least two trips, using a box.

Father Dowling, having lit his pipe and puffed up half a roomful of smoke, got up from his chair and went back to the kitchen. Marie Murkin followed him. He stopped in the middle of the room and stared at the floor.

"Two," he said. "So they could do it in one trip."

He was looking at the tracking across her floor, from door to basement entrance and back again. They hadn't wiped their feet at all. She brought out her mop from the basement hallway. Father Dowling looked as if he might stop her, but then he didn't. While she cleaned up the mess, he went back to his study. He had turned away from his desk and was staring out the window, puffing on his pipe, when she came back.

"I'm going to call Captain Keegan."

"No, Marie. Don't."

"Father Dowling . . ." she began.

He turned and looked at her with a faint smile. "For one thing, he has gone into Chicago for the day. For another, it's not that important."

"Do you realize how much jam and jelly there was down there?"

"I meant it's not important to the police. Of course it's important to you. And to the parish."

"What am I supposed to prepare for dinner? Nothing's defrosted."

"Marie, anything you make is fine with me."

"I haven't any meat."

"Something meatless, then. After all, it is Lent."

"I haven't anything meatless. I'll have to go to the store."

He commiserated with her, even offered to go for her, but she was having none of that. Besides, it was like punishing him for not calling the police to deprive him of the chance to do her a favor.

"Why don't you go out the front way," he said, when she had on her coat and hat.

"My car's out back."

He opened the front door and stood there and then she understood. Of course. He would want to go look for a trail away from the back door. She stepped inside and closed the front door.

"Let's both look, Father."

Mrs. Murkin kept her back porch free of snow, going at it with a broom whenever the wind blew drifts of snow across the porch floor. The sidewalk leading to the church was also clean of snow, thanks to Feeney, or thanks to her nagging Feeney, depending on how you wanted to look at it. Mrs. Murkin didn't want Father Dowling to have to plow through snow on his way to Mass. He refused to wear rubbers and he was susceptible to colds and she didn't want him sniffling around the house making her feel guilty for not having kept germs from the rectory door.

So there was nothing to see on the porch or sidewalk. But they hadn't taken the sidewalk. Fresh footprints trailed across the snow-covered yard toward the street. They led to where a pickup truck was parked. Marie Murkin stepped back from the edge of the porch.

"They're still there," she whispered.

"Nonsense."

"The trail goes right to that truck."

"It goes to the street. The truck is empty. Who knows how long it's been there?"

"That's what I mean. I'm calling the police."

She turned to go inside but Father Dowling took her arm. "Marie, get out your car and go do your shopping."

"Sure. And as soon as I'm gone you'll go out and take a look in that truck."

"Don't be silly."

"You will and you know it. Well, I'm going to do it now."

And off she marched, a wiry little woman ready to take on the world of thieves and bandits. She had put on her overshoes—she wasn't too proud to admit that she could catch cold if she waded around in snow wearing only shoes—so she just left the sidewalk and walked beside the trail that led to the truck. She was halfway to it when she realized Father Dowling was following her. She turned and actually shook a finger at him.

"Father Dowling, you go back. This snow is nearly a foot deep."

But he kept coming and the only way she could have stopped him was by making a spectacle of herself. Besides, it had been her idea, going to look at the truck, so who was to blame? She sighed and resumed her walk.

The truck was empty, and there was no one visible in the cab. Mrs. Murkin looked in the back, but there was no sign of the stolen food. She kept on going around the truck—she was in no mood for any I-told-you-so's—out into the street and up to the driver's side of the cab. She stood on tiptoe and, shading the window with a gloved hand, looked inside.

That was the third thing.

The man lay across the seat, face down, his head on his arm, and at first she thought he was asleep. But then she saw that his eye was open. His mouth was too. But it was the blood that told her the man was dead. He lay in a pool of it and it was spattered around the cab too. Even the window she looked through, she now realized, was smeared with it.

Her voice rose like a siren into the thin winter air and she stumbled back from the truck and might have collapsed right there in the street if Father Dowling had not come running to break her fall.

"Call Captain Keegan," she cried, and then she did fall, dreamily, into the dark.

2

PHIL KEEGAN had not gone to Chicago as he had told Roger
Dowling he would. The trip was a routine matter, anyone could
do it. Besides, this was his day off and, almost as a Lenten pen-
ance, he decided to spend the afternoon at home.

Home. Home was an apartment in a new development
along the river, a mix of four-story buuildings and town houses
featuring mansard roofs and clustered around an artificial lake
in which indolent ducks floated during four seasons of the year.
Standing at the glass doors that gave onto his balcony, Phil
Keegan looked down at the ducks without affection. He felt a
small and grudging admiration for the way they kept pecking
away at the ice, keeping a small expanse of open water in which
to swim, but their quacking, accusative and plaintive, annoyed
him as much as ever. The ducks were spoiled. The inhabitants

of the development fed them to a fault, so that now the jaded fowl had to be persuaded to taste the delicacies brought to them. It was damned nonsense to create an artificial lake within twenty-five yards of the river. Why didn't the buildings face the river instead of the man-made lake? It was a visitor from the river that held Keegan's attention now.

A mallard had swept in over some trees at the far end of the lake and come in for a landing on the iced-over surface. Was it fanciful to think he created confusion among the pampered ducks bobbing on the water? Maybe one species of bird can't even see members of another species. The mallard might have been Keegan himself; he felt equally out of place in his apartment. But there had been no point in keeping the house after his wife had died. His daughters were married and living elsewhere in the country, leaving Keegan all alone. This was something he managed to forget by working hard and, in his off hours, spending as little time as he could in this apartment. And as much time as possible with Roger Dowling. Having a priest for best friend was different; certainly a lot of people in the department thought so, practically everyone except Cy Horvath. Keegan had, in his youth, wanted to be a priest. He had briefly attended Quigley, the archdiocesan preparatory seminary, and it was there he had first come to know Roger Dowling, who was in the class ahead of his. Latin had done Keegan in, he simply could not master it, and finally, on the advice of his spiritual advisor, he had thrown in the towel.

After the service, where he had served as an MP, he went through the academy on an accelerated program for veterans and joined the Fox River police department. Over the years he had risen to captain of detectives, raised his family, loved his wife, been content with his life. The kids grew up and left and then, a tragedy he had never foreseen, his wife died and he was alone. It was then, like that mallard, that he had moved into this spanking new development and an apartment he did not like. So he spent as little time there as he could. Roger Dowling's appointment to Fox River had been a godsend for Phil Keegan. He did not like to think what his life would be like without those evenings of cribbage in the rectory or following the Cubs with his old friend.

Take some time off. Relax. Enjoy yourself. This was the kind of advice he got more than he liked. It was well meant but he heard it as invitations to boredom, loneliness, self-pity. He swung away from the window. To hell with it. He wasn't going to mope around the apartment feeling sorry for himself. The sound of the phone was like a reprieve and he picked it up before the first ring ended. It was Horvath.

"Something funny over at Saint Hilary's, Captain."

"Tell me. I like a good laugh."

There was silence on the other end of the line. Keegan closed his eyes and shook his head. It was a dumb thing to say, and uncharacteristic. A couple of hours at home and he was going stir crazy.

Horvath said, "I don't mean funny. Strange. There's a body in a pickup parked in front of the parish house."

"Dowling call it in?"

"Yes."

"Who is it?"

"A car is on its way out there. He just called."

"I'll meet you there. And Cy?"

"What?"

"Thanks for calling me."

Horvath knew how close he was to Roger Dowling; even more, Cy knew how much he hated to be sitting home doing nothing. The thought of retirement made Keegan physically ill. He had the years in now; he could go on pension. He would rather face a firing squad. Having gotten into his coat and pulled on his hat, he left the apartment and bounced down the stairs. To hell with the elevator. He realized he was whistling. He stopped himself. A body had been found. As Cy said, that wasn't funny. But then why did he feel so damned good as he pushed through the door of his building and half ran, half skated to his car?

The sight of the ambulance when he drew up in front of the rectory suggested to Keegan that the body had not been a dead one, but Horvath corrected that impression.

"It's for Mrs. Murkin."

"Did something happen to her?" Keegan was surprised by the catch in his voice.

"She fainted."

"Oh."

"Father Dowling insisted on her being looked at. I don't think she'll ever forgive him."

"Yeah," Keegan said, and went up the walk to the house. "Is that the truck there?"

There was no answer. Horvath was not following him, but going to the pickup where the lab technicians were doing their stuff. Good idea. Keegan let himself into the rectory and was surprised to find Roger Dowling alone in his study.

"How's Marie?" Keegan asked.

"I didn't think they'd call an ambulance. They actually carried her out of the house into the ambulance. To examine her. Oh, the look she gave me when she came back in."

"She in the kitchen?"

"I think she's gone up to her room. If you want a beer, help yourself."

In the kitchen, Keegan looked at the closed door of the staircase that led up to the housekeeper's room. He had half a mind to open it and call up to Mrs. Murkin, but that would have been teasing, and if Roger was right she was in no mood.

He opened a bottle of beer and took it back to the study where he slumped into a leather chair.

"How was Chicago, Phil?"

"I didn't go."

Roger said nothing further, perhaps he sensed how it had been with Keegan, trying to relax and take it easy. What would the priest think of his elation that a dead body had won him freedom from relaxation? Keegan frowned and asked Father Dowling to tell him just what had happened.

"I don't know, Phil. We went out to the truck and Mrs. Murkin looked into the cab and there was the body."

"The truck looked suspicious?"

"No."

"Then why did you go out there?"

"Mrs. Murkin was going to the store."

"You were going with her?" Keegan asked, surprised.

Dowling struck a match and held the flame over the bowl of his pipe. His thin face grew thinner as his cheeks hollowed. The flame dipped into the bowl and smoke began to emerge from the priest's mouth.

"It began with the money box in the church."

Keegan sat forward. "What do you mean?"

Dowling told the story almost apologetically. "I am only bothering you with this because Marie Murkin wanted me to call you right away. Imagine that she is telling you this."

"Okay. So someone took money from the magazine rack. How much?"

"It couldn't be much."

"Two dollars, three, what?"

"It could have been twenty-five, but I doubt it. Perhaps half that. And they ruined the box. Well, that's the end of that. From now on all the stuff in the back of the church will be free for the taking."

"It sounds as if it already was."

"That is the first theft, Phil."

"Not counting being short-changed? What did you mean, it began with the money box?"

"Then there was the jam and jelly. And pork chops."

"Tell me about it."

Listening, Phil Keegan reminded himself that he was to imagine it was Marie Murkin telling him this, but that didn't help much. This kind of narrative could include mention of just about anything that had gone on in the rectory today.

"That's not fair, Phil. It was another theft."

"Maybe she hadn't brought up the pork chops from the freezer before taking her nap."

"All her jam and jelly is gone. And she had brought up the pork chops. You could see that from the condition of the drain board where they were defrosting. And the thieves had tracked up her newly scrubbed floor."

"Thieves?"

"There were two of them."

Keegan stopped himself from asking how Roger Dowling knew that. The priest liked to play detective; he was pretty good at it too, but it seemed a bit silly turning his talent to something like some missing pork chops and jars of jelly.

"Somebody just walked in here while Mrs. Murkin was taking her nap and I was sitting here reading my office. I don't like that. Their tracks led out to the truck."

Keegan was aware of a sound behind him and he turned to see Marie Murkin in the doorway. She bobbed at him and seemed to avoid looking at Father Dowling.

"So you've already got a beer? Good."

"Father has been bringing me up to date, Marie."

"Two thefts and a dead body, Captain Keegan."

"How are you feeling?"

"I feel fine! I never felt better in my life. I slipped in the street and . . ."

"The ambulance is routine, Marie. The man might not have been dead. It is a man, isn't it?"

Marie Murkin's face paled and her eyes widened with the memory of what she had seen when she looked into the cab of that truck. For a moment, Keegan wondered if she was going to keel over. Is that what she had meant by slipping in the street?

"Haven't you discovered who he is?"

"They're checking on that now," Keegan said, assuming that was true. With Horvath out there, he could be sure everything would be done according to the book.

"Were you told about the other things?"

Father Dowling said, "I told him, Marie."

"Did they find my things?" Mrs. Murkin asked Keegan.

"What would that be?"

"Did they find my jars of jelly and the pork chops?"

"I'll let you know," Keegan said and, to get past the awkward moment, added, "Is there another beer in the kitchen, Marie?"

"Of course."

She turned to go, stopped, addressed a point above the pastor's head. "Can I get anything for you, Father?"

"No, thank you."

She sighed a martyr's sigh and then was gone.

3

MARCUS RIEHLE was one of Fox River's most widely read writers, and the least known. Not that being a Fox River writer put him in a crowded category; he kept close tabs on that, all right, showing up at the public library when the fortnightly meetings of the local writers club convened—not attending, you understand, just being there, eavesdropping, scouting the competition, most of it merely potential.

He was a small man in height and a large man in girth, a man whose glasses seemed to attract whatever light there was so that he turned an opaque expression on the world, reflective, though not quite in the sense of the term he would have liked to apply to himself. On this February night, browsing in reference books meant for engineers just outside the room the librarian made available to the writers club, Riehle took a surreptitious roll call.

Seven. Not bad. He smiled and his glasses glittered. A number like that gave much the same pleasure as finding that the average age in the obituary column added twenty-five to his own. Marcus Riehle was fifty-one. He scowled. If seven Fox River writers was a welcome number, fifty-one years of age was not. Better to concentrate on the poor turnout. Mrs. Ennis, needless to say, was there, "in the chair" as she would put it, trying to transplant to the recalcitrant cultural soil of Illinois the lore and jargon of her overweening Anglophilia. (Riehle honed such descriptive phrases as these to imagined perfection in his mind. "A writer is writing every conscious minute," he would have said in the public lecture on his calling that he had never been asked to deliver.) Mrs. Ennis might have been expected to welcome him to the club and provide the forum in which Riehle might at last enunciate the jeweled phrases that sang in his mind, but he had never given her the opportunity. And he never would. He stuttered.

It was his cross, his tragic flaw, his goad. Would he have resolved to become a writer if he had been able to express himself orally with facility? Perhaps. Other writers had the gift of gab as well as a golden pen. But, in his own case, Marcus Riehle was all but certain that his speech impediment had determined him to master his mother tongue in the silent form of writing. He had come a long and rocky road, and it was not the road he had planned to come along. Take this for a measure, it said it all: Mrs. Ennis would not know who he was. His name would be unfamiliar to her. She would not even suspect he was Fox River's most prolific author.

Riehle was a native of Fox River. He had attended St. Hilary grade school, gone on to Hixon Military Academy, and thence into the service, where he was assigned to something rather mystifyingly called Intelligence. Until he was assigned to *Stars and Stripes*. He had not realized this was actually an intelligence assignment and he had been captivated by the excitement and self-importance of journalism. So he used the GI Bill at Bradley, entering as a journalism major, but switching to English when his calling became clear to him.

Marcus Riehle, writer. When did that legend first go up in lights in the private theater of his imagination? Not, as one might have thought, because of some course in English, nor as a result of a protreptic lecture in his creative writing class. It had happened in a drugstore when his eye alighted on a magazine for writers. To this day he could recall the skepticism with which he had taken the magazine from the rack. He had leafed through it and his disdainful smile soon faded. At the soda fountain counter he had two cherry Cokes and read a third of the magazine. His pulse was racing. Was it possible that what he sought in vain on a college campus was readily available here among the shampoos and medicines and Lucky Strikes? He walked from the store in a daze, only to have a hand laid on his shoulder before he reached the curb.

"You wanna pay me for the magazine, Fatso?"

Even if he had not been startled, he would have been unable to defend himself against the accusation. He had long ago learned not to reply, or try to reply, to the sudden remark, the unexpected question. If speak he must, it was better to initiate it, take his time, get into control of the conversation. Now he looked into the sarcastic expression on the pharmacist's face. The man was not exactly underweight himself, as Riehle would scathingly observe when he replayed this scene later in the privacy of his room.

"Tell me you forgot."

Riehle nodded, not fighting it, and drew out his wallet. He checked the cover of the magazine for the price. Luckily, he had the exact change. The pharmacist refused to take it. Hands on his hips, head to one side, he was obviously enjoying dealing with so spineless a shoplifter. Riehle thrust the money at him.

"Cat got your tongue?"

"T-t-t-take the goddamn money," Riehle blurted out, dropping the coins into the pocket of the pharmacist's jacket. The fire in his frustrated eye sent the pharmacist scooting back into his store.

That should have destroyed the mood reading the magazine had induced in him, but it did not. The humiliating encounter with the pharmacist on the public sidewalk added to the significance of the discovery he had made. The memory of the taunting druggist was a spur, the man became a symbol of all those who must be shown the mettle of Marcus Riehle. He read the magazine ragged, he let its confident prose and promissory ads overwhelm his doubts, he became convinced that within weeks, with determination, with discipline, he would burst like a meteor across the literary skies. Marcus Riehle, writer. Nonfiction or fiction? Fiction, of course. The novelist and writer of short stories were figures of romance and glamour, often tragic figures given to drink, profligacy, and femmes fatales. Riehle himself could not tolerate alcohol, he was niggardly with money, and as for women, well, the only coed who showed interest in him was a girl with frizzy hair who weighed two hundred pounds and lisped. To respond to her overtures would have been too much like self-mockery. But it was talent rather than authorial flaws that Riehle lacked.

There were times when he himself marveled at the tenacity with which he had stuck to his typewriter during the ten lean years when he had proved beyond the shadow of a doubt that he was not a writer of short stories, or of novels either. He wrote hundreds of the former and two and a half of the latter. He still had all his manuscripts—first drafts, revisions, final copy in duplicate, the carbon he had kept and the ribbon copy that had gone the rounds of the editorial offices. Three four-drawer file cabinets were required to hold this monument to misguided effort.

Having failed at fiction, Riehle turned to fact, but he was not to find his groove for yet another decade. This time inspiration came when he had sunk to the depths of despair. Reversal after reversal, supporting himself with jobs a self-respecting high school student would have scorned—bag boy at a supermarket, clerk in a twenty-four-hour dairy store, part of a street repair crew with the city—eventually even Marcus Riehle ran out of optimism. Was it possible that he was radically mistaken about himself? Was his certainty that he was destined to make his mark as a writer entirely unfounded? He was tempted by pornography, studying a Chicago publisher's ad, a flat fee of two hundred and fifty dollars for a dirty book; he bought a few examples and paged sheepishly through them. He tore them into pieces before throwing them away. And he went off to confession to rid himself of the guilt he felt at having sullied his soul with such garbage.

Having whispered his sins through the grill and received absolution, Marcus Riehle knelt in a pew in St. Hilary's church, a place familiar to him from childhood, and put his face into his hands. He wept over his life that seemed a futile joke. What had he accomplished since he had knelt in this church as a child? Nothing. Nothing. The tears cleansed his heart as confession had his soul, and his prayer—Lord, what should I do?—was answered as he left the church. He dipped his fingers into the holy water font and as he brought them to his forehead he saw the magazine rack.

Within a year Marcus Riehle had written sixty-three pamphlets. His talent, it turned out, was for writing uplifting prose of a more or less nondenominational sort. He was his own publisher. After he had written his first pamphlet, he took it to a printer and then ran ads in the classified sections of a dozen religious papers. The response was by any reckoning remarkable and, compared with the years of unalleviated failure through which he had come, seemed to Marcus Riehle a veritable sign from heaven. He followed his first success with another and another, each more impressive than the previous one. His ads moved out of classified and became quarter page, half page, full page in color. He prospered. He rented a list of parish priests and offered discount prices for bulk sales. Again the response was phenomenal. One priest canceled his order because the pamphlets contained no imprimatur. Marcus Riehle never made that mistake again. Each of his pamphlets bore the imprimatur of a bishop in New Mexico who would have been surprised to learn he had granted it. The likelihood of that was slim. Riehle never filled an order from New Mexico.

The day he saw his writings in the pamphlet rack at St. Hilary's parish he felt he had fulfilled his destiny. He was a writer. He was a publisher. He was prospering. He lived by his pen. No member of the Fox River writers club could make that statement, least of all Mrs. Ennis. Why, then, on this February night, as he had so often before, did he linger outside the meeting room as if he were the aspirant and Mrs. Ennis and her flock the proven professionals? Why couldn't he just march in there and tell them who he was?

Because he stuttered.

He had written Mrs. Ennis a letter. She had not answered. How could she? He had signed a false name and given no return address. Riehle had the crazy conviction that if she ever looked him straight in the eye she would recognize in him the man who had professed his undying love for her.

"What's going on in there?" someone whispered at his elbow, the breath redolent of alcohol. Riehle started and turned guiltily to the man who had spoken.

"Some meeting." He whispered, hardly sounding the words. In this fashion he could speak.

"What kind?"

"Writers." He had to mouth it several times before the man understood. Riehle recognized the unshaven man as one of the quasi-vagrants who spent much of the winter day lounging about the library's reading rooms.

"Who's the broad?"

Riehle turned away, chivalrously ignoring this disrespectful allusion to Mrs. Ennis. He walked rapidly to the front of the library and, when he pushed through the gate on his way out, set off an alarm. He still held the reference book that had been his decoy for spying on Mrs. Ennis. A security man sprang from the chair he sat in, exultant at this infrequent chance to fulfill his role. A blush suffused Riehle's cheek and he reached back over the gate and dropped the book on the checkout desk.

"Did you want to borrow that?" the librarian asked, exchanging an enigmatic look with the security man.

Riehle shook his head and tried to speak, "F-f-f-f . . ."

A hand closed on his arm and he was pulled toward the door by the security man, who hissed in his ear, "Watch what you say, buddy. I mean it."

A moment later Riehle found himself on the sidewalk with a cold wind whipping his clothes. He had been treated like a thief. His inability to tell the librarian to forget it had been taken as an effort at obscenity.

Putting his hands into his pockets, the fingers of his right hand closing around the loose money it found, he dipped his head and set off into the wind.

4

Lieutenant Cyril Horvath was a huge man, in many ways an ugly man, yet he was also someone others instinctively trusted and someone whom women liked. Liked and trusted. In his taciturnity he had, as well, the look of a man who knows more about you than it is comfortable to have known. His silence and his receptive expression made him the confidant of many. In his line of work, this effortless ability to elicit information from people was one of Horvath's principal assets. That and his reliability. Phil Keegan had implicit and justified trust in Cy Horvath.

"Wasn't there any information on the body?" Keegan asked him.

"Sure."

"Well?"

Horvath was used to Keegan's manner. The captain always wanted everything done at once, and done well. Horvath shared what he took to be the source of Keegan's impatience. A crime in Fox River was like a personal insult. How dare a thief or a con artist or pusher presume to ply his trade within the area of responsibility of Phil Keegan? Or of Cy Horvath, for that matter. Until the area was cleansed again, neither man could really relax. So Horvath understood Keegan's impatience to know the identity of the man whose dead body had been found in the pickup parked on the street outside St. Hilary's rectory. That was an added factor, of course. Roger Dowling was the pastor of St. Hilary. It was further insult that a body shot full of holes should be deposited outside the residence of Phil Keegan's old friend Father Dowling.

"He had half a dozen sets of identification, none that looks genuine."

"The truck?"

"Not his."

"Stolen?"

"It wasn't reported. We're looking into that."

"We?"

This was the question Horvath had dreaded. "I sent Peanuts out to—"

"Pianone!"

"There wasn't anyone else. I've been checking out all this phony ID the guy had on him."

Keegan wiped his face with the palm of his hand. Bad as Pianone was, they had to make use of him, not just because his family had been in politics in Fox River for over a quarter of a century, swilling at the public trough, but because budgetary cutbacks prevented the hiring of new men to replace those who retired. Horvath decided to give Keegan the whole story now.

"I sent Agnes with Peanuts."

Keegan, standing behind his desk, reached for the back

of his chair, as if to steady himself. Agnes Lamb was a black woman who had come onto the force six months earlier, insisting that she wanted, in her own words, combat duty. Money had been found by the Council to hire her. Her presence had given Keegan the sense that he was presiding over the fall of Western civilization. It was nothing personal. Or racist. Just sexist. Keegan just did not accept the idea of women cops.

"It used to be called chivalry," he growled to Horvath. "Now it's called chauvinism."

Horvath nodded. Keegan didn't expect him to reply.

"Women are to be protected. They're not protectors."

During that conversation, they had been having a beer in the Foxy Lounge and all Horvath had to do was listen and sip his beer. Keegan assumed that Cy agreed with him. And at that time he did, more or less. He really did not have any theory about women the way Keegan apparently did. Not protectors? Cy Horvath's mother had been his protector until he got big enough to protect himself. In the case of Agnes, Cy wondered if the fact that she was black had something to do with Keegan's attitude.

"It has a lot to do with her appointment, Cy."

"Maybe."

"No maybe about it. Robertson told me. A woman and a black, a real parlay in affirmative action."

"Maybe she'll work out."

"She will work, I guarantee you that."

Keegan worked her to the edge of unfairness, but Agnes worked out too and Cy Horvath had come to know and like her. As a cop. And as a person. She had been brought up tough, her childhood had exposed her to all sorts of things kids shouldn't have to know about. Cy considered his own upbringing a rough one, but Agnes had him beat a mile in that department. And she was a fighter. One of her half-brothers had been knifed in a rumble and died of his wounds. Agnes decided to do something about it.

"You are the enemy," she said to Cy. "I mean we are. Cops. Think of what that means. If the law is the enemy, the crook is the hero. The hustler, the pimp, the pusher, people like that are looked up to. No more. That has got to change. The law is ours too and you don't need to be a genius to see we need its protection."

"A crusader," Keegan had grumped when Cy told him of this.

"She's okay."

"Not as a cop," Keegan insisted, and you could see a door in his mind slam shut.

"I can find out about the truck if you want," Horvath said now.

"From Agnes and Peanuts? I want to know who the dead guy was."

"We should be hearing about his prints."

And they would be hearing about the autopsy too, when Phelps decided to tell them. The coroner was a man of glacial prudence. But when they learned who the man had been and how he had died, the real job remained. The autopsy would not put it this way, but the guy had been murdered. Killed. Some degree of murder or manslaughter the prosecutor would decide on once they got hold of the man who had pulled the trigger.

"A .22 pistol," Keegan mused. He had pulled his chair out and sat down. Horvath remained standing on the other side of the desk. "No wonder he emptied the damned thing into the guy. What are our chances of finding the weapon?"

"We'll find it," Cy said, his voice expressionless.

Keegan looked at him, then nodded. "You're right. But when?"

"That depends on where the shooting took place."

Horvath was guessing that the man had not been shot right there next to St. Hilary's rectory. The time of death was not as accurately computed as it might have been because the body had been out in the winter cold, but a fair guess put the time at six in the morning. The .22 might not strike Keegan or himself as all that lethal a weapon, as hand guns go, but it made a hell of a noise and Horvath just did not believe that so many shots could have been taken—the whole clip—without Roger Dowling hearing them. And when you added in Mrs. Murkin the housekeeper, well, the idea that all that noise could have gone unheard was out. For that matter, Horvath wasn't assuming the shooting had taken place in the truck.

"He's shot, then dumped into the truck, and the killer drives him to Saint Hilary's, parks the truck, and walks away?" Keegan's voice got heavier with doubt as he spoke.

"The truck could have been hauled there."

"You mean by a wrecker?"

"Maybe. By another vehicle."

"What are you going on?"

Chain marks on the bumper, underneath a disturbance of ice and rust. The truck had been recently towed, there wasn't any doubt of that. And it hadn't been a professional job either, or it had been made to look like an amateur job, take your choice. You also had to take your choice as to whether the two took place on an earlier occasion or at the time of the transportation of the body to St. Hilary's.

"But why?" Keegan asked.

"Why haul it?"

"Why haul it there, to Saint Hilary's? What's the significance of that?"

"It's a quiet street."

"There are lots of quiet streets."

"That depends on how much time you have to choose one."

Neither man liked this sort of unanchored chatter. No theories. That was Keegan's motto of investigation, and Horvath agreed with him. But it was only an ideal. You were bound to imagine how things had happened and sometimes it helped. It was the times when it didn't that reminded you to be skeptical of the premature account of how things had come about. To get locked into the little scenario Cy had just sketched would be a mistake. The shooting *could* have occurred in the cab of the truck and while it was parked where they had found it. Horvath found that hard to believe, but he wasn't excluding it forever and ever.

Keegan's phone rang and he picked it up. His brows lifted and his eyes crossed as he looked across at Horvath, indicating that he should stand by.

"What have you got, Agnes?" Keegan said sweetly into the phone.

He nodded as he listened, got rid of the funny expression, picked up a pencil and began to write.

"Okay, okay. That's good." Keegan's eyes drifted away from Horvath. "Good work. Keep at it. Peanuts with you? Don't let him get run over." He hung up.

"Whose truck is it?" Horvath asked.

Keegan frowned at what he had written on a pad. When he looked at Horvath, there was an odd expression in his eyes. Amusement, surprise, pique, it would have been difficult to say.

"It was stolen from a lot on Curzon Road. Secondhand dealer."

"How long had he had it?"

"Agnes was complaining about his records."

"What's the dealer's name?"

"Liberati."

Keegan might have dealing the joker onto his desktop. Liberati? Geez. "How long has Liberati been in the used-truck business?"

"Check that out."

Now. Leaving Keegan's office, Horvath repressed the thought that it was going a little far afield to check out the dealer from whose lot had been stolen the pickup in which the dead body had been found. It was far too soon to tell what was the main line and what was the tangent.

But Horvath wished they knew who the dead man was.

5

IN THE offices of Tuttle & Tuttle the eponymous Tuttle was worried. He had no client, a state of affairs sufficient to induce anxiety in the most intrepid of lawyers. In one like Tuttle, for whom a law degree represented a license to enrich himself at the expense of his clients and little else, it was catastrophic to be sitting here, tweed hat pulled over his eyes, feet on his desk, the police band purring in his ear from the portable radio he had planted among the debris on his desk. The radio needed fresh batteries. And so do I, thought Tuttle. In the outer office, his secretary-receptionist's typewriter had fallen silent. He had no work for her and an hour before, passing her desk, he had heard the hum of her machine.

"Turn that damned thing off."

"It doesn't cost that much," she said sassily.

"Turn it off! You turn everyone and everything else off, turn off the goddamn machine."

A mistake that, he could admit it to himself. But when Delphine leaped to her feet and, grabbing her purse, brought it in a great sweeping arc in the direction of Tuttle's head, he had ducked into his office and shut the door. Through its panels, through the flimsy wall separating outer from inner office, her abuse had been audible for ten minutes. Finally Tuttle had plugged his ears so as not to hear the endless indictment of himself as boss, as lawyer, as human being. He had had no idea what a seething caldron of resentment Delphine was. But then her paycheck had bounced last Friday and her loyalty had been further strained by Tuttle's suggestion that she save herself a little income tax by taking a week off without pay. When her tirade was done and she had slammed out of the office, he wondered if she would ever come back. Worse, he wondered if he would ever need her again. Two weeks with nothing more promising than a court appointment to defend a woman who had driven around town with a load of bricks that she systematically heaved through the windows of dirty book stores. Tuttle had momentarily seen his name all over the front page on that one, but when he learned the woman's notion of dirty books the hope faded. She had put one brick through the plate-glass window of a Christian Science reading room that had a Bible on display. She was only a nut after all.

Suddenly his ear cocked at the radio and he dragged his feet off the desk, picked up the portable, and held it to his ear. The volume dropped as he did this. He stood and, with the radio pressed to the side of his head, turned slowly, trying to pick up the signal more clearly, using his body as an antenna. But the sound dropped to inaudibility. Damn. He raised the radio high but throught better of smashing it to the floor. He was sure he had heard correctly.

His face gathered about his nose as he gave himself up to thought, puckering, eyes squeezed shut, lips pushed out and brought up under his nostrils, chin pulled in. He might have been tuned to a more ethereal broadcast than his radio could supply. His face relaxed, his eyes opened and sparkled. He had it. He sat, picked up the phone, and knew a half second's panic before the buzz filled his ear. His phone had been cut off in the past; he knew it could happen. He dialed and was answered almost immediately.

"Officer Pianone, please."

"Who's calling?"

"Is he there?"

"He's on an investigation."

"I know. This is Tuttle, the attorney. It is imperative that I get through to Pianone immediately. Can you patch me through to him?"

"I'll take your number."

Tuttle sullenly gave his number to the police operator. Didn't she recognize him? Perhaps she did and that was the problem. But they should have his number there, for quick consultation. He brushed the thought away. Never dwell on negative facts. Accentuate the positive. There was a tune to that which Tuttle could hum off key. He realized that the police operator had hung up. He put his phone down quickly. He didn't want Peanuts getting a busy signal. Peanuts could not be counted on to keep trying until he got through. Call Tuttle. He would take it literally, do it once and then forget it. Nonetheless, Peanuts was worth his weight in gold as far as Tuttle was concerned. The police band had its uses, but Peanuts was Tuttle's entree into what was going on down at police headquarters, particularly in the detective division presided over by Captain Phil Keegan.

Peanuts did not phone. He dropped by and he had a

black woman with him. Tuttle's eyes widened when Agnes Lamb was identified as a cop.

"Finally," Tuttle cried. "It's about time they started hiring minorities."

Agnes did not respond as Tuttle had hoped—not that he considered himself all that expert at reading black expressions. He found this woman enigmatic and he wished Peanuts hadn't brought her along.

Agnes said, "We got a call you wanted to see us?"

Tuttle allowed his mouth to drop open, then gave an unconvincing performance of a man vastly amused. His phony laughter bounced off his office walls. "Don't tell me they bothered you with a thing like that when you were on duty, Peanuts." He laughed some more. "I just wanted to invite you out for dinner tonight. Chinese."

At the prospect of Chinese food, Peanuts' expression altered and Tuttle half expected saliva to become visible at the corners of his mouth. Peanuts would sell anyone but a relative for a plateful of chicken chow mein. Peanuts glanced at his watch. His wrist was so large that the band of his watch, eating into the flesh, looked as if it must stop circulation to the fingers.

"What time you got now?" Peanuts asked.

"It's after four," Officer Lamb said. She managed to keep a straight face. "I could leave you here and take the car into the garage, okay?"

"But I'm driving," Peanuts said, and his brow dipped as he looked petulantly at his fellow officer. "I'll take you downtown."

"You could drop me at home," she said sweetly.

Tuttle intervened. He opined that Agnes's first suggestion was the wiser. As for Peanuts, he did not think he could postpone dinner until he had deposited Agnes and returned. Not while he was thinking of the egg roll at the Nankin, he couldn't. That did it. Peanuts wiped at the corners of his mouth with the back of one hand while he fished the car keys from his pocket with the other. Agnes took them but did not immediately leave.

"You're a lawyer, right?"

The walls were covered with law books. "You keep that up and they gonna make you a detective. Am I a lawyer or am I not, Peanuts?"

Peanuts stood there as if he were waiting for the doubt to be resolved. Tuttle chuckled through clenched teeth and punched Peanuts on the arm. To Agnes he said, "You ever need a lawyer, you come to me, young lady."

"I'm not on that side of the law, Mr. Tuttle."

"Now, now. A lawyer does many things. Everybody needs a lawyer sooner or later. Even lawyers do."

Agnes Lamb seemed doubtful of the universal need for legal representation, but the main thing was to get her on her way and take Peanuts to the Nankin and pump him about the mention of Liberati on the police band.

6

WHAT HAD once been the St. Hilary parish school had been converted into a center where the adults of the parish could gather, during the day but also in the evening, to pursue various arts and crafts, to play cards and, two nights a week, bingo, or just to reminisce about the good old days. A disproportionate number of the parishioners were elderly, which is why it had made sense to use the building for them rather than for the few children of school age still living within the boundaries of St. Hilary's parish. Edna Hospers was in charge, providing not only a variety of activities, but the attention many of these men and women no longer received from their own children.

Father Dowling went over to the school the day after the body was found in the pickup truck. He would have dropped by in any case, but Edna had phoned the rectory and pleaded with him to come early.

"It is *the* topic of conversation, Father, and they'd like to get the story from you."

"They would learn more from reading the *Messenger,* Edna, but of course I'll come. Tell them not to get their hopes too high. I don't know much more about it than they do."

Edna was not in her office when he entered the school. Once a nun would have been ensconced there, the principal, her countenance ringed by starched linen, and in the rooms lining the corridor there would have been the murmur of children learning. It was the sort of thing that could prompt Phil Keegan to lengthy lamentation, a dirge for what was no more. Roger Dowling regretted the passing of many things, but the demise of the parish school was the result of demographic changes in Fox River, not changes in the Church. People fled to the suburbs, abandoning the city. A triangle of land contained St. Hilary's parish, a triangle formed by Interstates that were the concrete conduits of suburbanites who twice a day roared along them going to or from Chicago. It was the disappearance of a school-age population, not some putative result of Vatican II, that had turned a school into a day-care center for aging adults.

Most likely Edna was in what had been the gym. Roger Dowling did not go immediately in search of her. His eye was caught by the church and rectory framed in the window of Edna's office. The large lovely church witnessed to a more prosperous period in the parish history, and the rectory too was an attractive structure. Father Dowling saw them through a blur of affection. Home. The parish had been selected as his exile and it had become his home.

There had been a time when it was common wisdom that Roger Dowling was destined to become a bishop. He had a doctorate in canon law from the Catholic University, he was an important presence on the archdiocesan marriage court. Whatever his own future prospects, his days were filled with the anguish of men and women seeking a way out of their marriages. Some of these requests were unserious, more were motivated by nothing weightier than what leads to the average civil divorce. It was the rest who represented tragedy, a marital cul-de-sac, an insoluble problem. Roger Dowling found that he could not simply process cases. It was not only the fact that the answer to the basic question put to the court must almost always be No. It was the spectacle of all these people caught in the web of their own promises, self-bound. Most of them knew in advance that there was no hope, that their suit was futile, a gesture. And yet to make that gesture was to introduce another negative factor into their lives. How can a marriage one has tried to get out of remain unaffected by the attempt?

Roger Dowling found himself anguishing along with those who came before him, but it was an anguish he could not display. To make manifest his sympathy might create a hope he had no right to encourage. He began to drink. Socially at first, then privately too; finally he drank almost exclusively in solitude. Under the psychological pressure of his job, the unvented empathy he felt for those who came before the court, he drank steadily and for a long time undetected. Then came blackouts and missed days. When finally he went off to a sanitarium in Wisconsin that catered to clerical alcoholics, he had not only drunk himself out of his job on the marriage court; any prospect of clerical advancement was gone forever. Dried out, he was assigned as pastor to St. Hilary, a parish in Fox River, a town to the west of Chicago.

Siberia. Ultima Thule. Exile. That is what St. Hilary's meant in clerical circles, and Roger Dowling's assignment was greeted with sad smiles and that far-off look with which one receives news of the fall of friends. Hunniker, Roger Dowling's predecessor as pastor, had been a jock and a bit of a figure of fun; he had been felled by a stroke while working out with bar bells in the basement of the rectory. Between his tenure and Roger Dowling's, the parish had been tossed back and forth between several religious orders. Roger Dowling reclaimed the parish, so to speak, but few would have regarded this as an accomplishment. The Franciscans, it was said, were relieved to unload St. Hilary's. When Roger Dowling took possession he had some of the feelings with which, he imagined, a lifer might inspect his cell.

He grew to like it, he came to love it, he realized that in His Providence God was giving him another chance. A failure? Of course he was a failure, a failure like those with whom he had commiserated at the marriage court, a failure like everyone else. Robert Louis Stevenson said that whatever we are meant to do, we are not meant to succeed. Failure is the human condition and there is only one remedy for it. So Roger Dowling rejoiced in his priesthood and in the role he could play among the people of his parish. He never drank again. He felt no desire for it. He was where he was meant to be and fully content with it, pastor of St. Hilary's, Fox River, Illiniois.

On his way down the corridor to the staircase that would take him to the gym, he became aware of an insistent sound. Tapping. Knocking. He stopped and cocked his head. And then he heard a woman's voice. He went to a door set between two lavatory entrances and pulled on the knob. Locked. He put his ear to the door.

"Who's in there?"

"Father Dowling, is that you?" Good Lord, it was Edna Hosper. "I'm locked in."

"Where is the key?"

"In my desk. The middle drawer. There is a bunch of keys with a piece of red yarn tied to the ring."

"I'll be right back."

"I'll be here," she said, trying for brightness, but her voice broke.

He found the keys without trouble and hurried back to the door. It took him some time to find the right key but finally he had it and turned it in the lock. Edna pushed out and came blinking into the light. Father Dowling took her elbow to steady her.

"What in the world were you doing in that closet?"

She shook her head, pressing her fingers against her closed eyes. "I can hardly see."

"Let's go to your office."

"I'll be all right."

"How did the door get locked?"

She looked at him as if considering what to say and then decided to say nothing. Roger Dowling did not pursue it. Her husband? The possibility decided him against demanding an explanation of how she had come to be locked in the closet.

"How long were you in there, Edna?"

"What time is it?"

He told her. "How long after we spoke on the phone?"

"Right after."

Ten minutes in there? Fifteen? However short a time, it must have seemed long. Poor Edna. Still he sensed, over and above her embarrassment, a reluctance to discuss this that went deep.

"So they want to hear about the body in the truck?" he said cheerily. "Let's go."

Edna came with him to the gym where Roger Dowling gave as matter-of-fact and non-sensational a presentation of what had happened as he could. He had meant it when he told Edna that people could learn more about it from the newspapers than from him. But what everyone really wanted was to talk about it and that meant questions that were largely statements of opinion Father Dowling was expected to endorse.

Little Mrs. Carr, stroking her upper lip with thumb and forefinger as if preening a mustache, squinted skeptically at Father Dowling.

"You left something out, Father."

"That's all I know."

"The name of the victim," Jennie Carr said triumphantly. "Who was the man in the truck?"

"Not even the police know that. At least they didn't the last time I talked with them."

"How can we figure it out if we don't know the name of the victim?"

"The police will take care of all that, Jennie."

"Oh, sure. The way they always do."

The next questioner had a taste for gore. How many shots? Where? Had there been a lot of bleeding? How long had the body been in the truck? There was an uncomfortable stirring among the old people.

"I think we should do what *we* can do. Say a prayer for the repose of his soul. You can remain seated."

Despite his remark, some struggled to their feet and got down on arthritic knees while Roger Dowling led them in the Lord's Prayer.

"One more for the person responsible for his death," he suggested.

They let him go then, perhaps fearful he would think of someone else to pray for. Edna, he noticed, had slipped away, apparently while he was talking with the old people about the body. At the door, Roger Dowling had a thought that struck him more forcibly because he wondered why he had not had it before. It may have been one of these old men or women who was responsible for Edna's being locked in that closet. His eyes roved over the several dozen oldsters who had gone back to what they had been doing earlier: a man sprinkled sawdust for shuffleboard, chairs at a bridge table were being reclaimed, the audio on the TV was adjusted upward to accommodate the hard of hearing. Like the very young, the very old can seem deceptively innocent, but Father Dowling knew that the mean, the bad, the evil deed can be performed by anyone and at any age.

As he stood there, Jennie Carr approached him. "There was another thing you left out, Father. The thief."

"How do you mean?"

"Money from the church, jelly from the parish house."

Smiling into Jennie Carr's knowing grin, Father Dowling wondered how she had learned of these things. He was certain no mention had been made of them in the newspaper account of an unidentified body found near St. Hilary's rectory.

"Who do you suppose did those things, Jennie?"

"I say it was an inside job."

"Inside what?"

"The parish! How would anyone know of Marie Murkin's jams and jellies without being a member of Saint Hilary's?"

"You may be right."

"But you don't think so?"

"We can't assume the same person stole the money from the church and broke into the parish house."

"I'm not! It could be two different people. I know that. But both of them are members of Saint Hilary's parish."

A corner of a paperback mystery emerged from the pocket of Jennie Carr's coat sweater. Father Dowling knew her to be an indefatigable reader of mystery novels, and she favored those that concentrated on events tied together by the tightest logical relations. Every event had its cause, nothing was without significance, a clue buried on page 4 would unlock the mystery on the penultimate page and show how, nesting box within box, the puzzle actually consisted of a sequence of inexorably related events. Father Dowling doubted that things look that way to God Himself, but if it pleased Jennie Carr to think that a clear mind and a little concentration would make any occurrence deliver up its necessity, it was a harmless sport.

"I must find Mrs. Hospers, Jennie," he said, turning to go.

"Is she lost again?"

The pale blue eyes glistened behind rimless glasses; white hair, parted in the middle, fell in gentle waves to just below Jennie's ears. She was stroking her upper lip with thumb and forefinger again.

"Again?"

She let go of her upper lip and clamped her hand over her mouth in a theatrical way. It was she who walked away from Father Dowling, after twenty feet stopping to look back at him over her shoulder, hand still clamped over her mouth. Naughty girl.

"Tell me about Jennie Carr," Roger Dowling said from the doorway of Edna's office. She sat behind her desk, turned in profile to him, one hand extended and lying on the telephone as if she had just hung up or was about to make a call or both.

"What has she done now, Father?"

He crossed the room to the desk. "Is she a bit of a troublemaker?"

"Oh, no. Nothing serious. She is a little different from the others. Brighter, for one thing, more with-it still."

"Edna, a wild question. Did Jennie Carr lock you in that closet?"

A sad smile formed slowly on Edna's lips. "A wild question and a lucky guess. How did you know?"

"Why would she do it?"

"Father, you really don't want to know all the trivial things that go on here."

"Don't I?"

"All right. She is a bad influence on people; she likes to stir up trouble. And there is a dear old man who has a terrible crush on her. She is merciless with him. He offers to do anything to prove his love and she sets him crazy tasks."

"Such as?"

Edna hesitated. "She's a little nasty too, Father."

"Edna, I had no idea you faced things like this. What nasty things does she make the old man do?"

Father Dowling had been a priest too long to be embarrassed or even surprised, but he did have to admit to himself as he walked back to the rectory that he would not have guessed what Jennie Carr had dared her suitor to do. Flashing was the word for it now, he believed; once it had simply been called indecent exposure. What old Carlo Liberati had been induced to by Jennie's dare was to walk through the gym wearing an open overcoat and nothing else except his shoes and socks.

"Captain Keegan called," Marie Murkin said when he was stamping snow from his shoes in the front hallway. "You didn't wear overshoes."

"I've just been over to the school."

Marie rolled her eyes. She was not sure she approved of having all those old people hanging around the school day after day. Not that she wasn't a great admirer of Edna Hospers.

"She's a saint, that woman, I don't mean otherwise. Nor do I blame the old people. But why do their families have to send them off every day like that, as if they were kids going to school? Honestly."

"Not all of them come every day, Marie."

"But some do. And if it were only one, it would be bad enough."

"They love it."

"That's because of Edna. She's a saint."

Phil Keegan, when Roger Dowling got through to him, had to be reminded that this was the return of his call. "If you're busy, we can talk later, Phil."

"No. Wait, Roger. I'm sorry. We know who the dead man is. I thought you'd want to know. Hingle. Enoch Hingle."

"That's an odd name."

"Oh, I don't know. You should have seen some of the names on his phony ID cards."

"Who was he?"

"A native of Chicago, but apparently he hasn't been seen around here in years. He had a scrape when he was young, car theft, but there's nothing on him more recent. The big surprise is that his body should show up in Fox River."

"How old was he?"

"He would have been forty in April."

"Any explanation?"

"Of what?"

Roger Dowling smiled. It was Phil Keegan's conviction that guesses should not be permitted to guide the routine of investigation. "I meant facts that would explain why he ended up here?"

"Nope. He was thought to have been living in the west."

"Where?"

"Oregon. Portland."

"What did he do there?"

"Well, he kept his nose clean after the early trouble in Chicago. At least he had no further trouble with the law. The Portland police draw a blank on him, and that includes all his aliases. Now it looks as if he was just lucky. You don't end up dead in that way if you've been a good boy."

"Why don't you stop by tonight, Phil?"

"I'll be there."

Over cribbage, Phil would tell him anything more they had learned of Enoch Hingle.

7

EVELYN CUNNINGHAM had trouble because of the snow, but she arrived at the adult center of St. Hilary's parish shortly after five. Snow had begun to fall as she made her way from the far side of town and now, waiting at the curb for her mother to come out, with the windshield wipers moving lazily back and forth brushing away the soft flakes that fluttered out of the darkness and enjoying a brief moment before dissolving and being swept away by the mesmeric movement of the blades, she gave herself up to thought. Often at this time, always when she realized that she found her mother only a burden, she felt melancholy, and the fleeting existence of the fallen flakes on the windshield seemed a metaphor of human life. Her mother's hold on life was tenacious, but Evelyn, as her fourth decade came to its end, felt that her own life was escaping her grasp at an ever-increasing rate.

Three husbands and a daughter, all behind her now, the daughter dead, the husbands divorced, she was now enjoying, if that was the right word, being alone again. Alone except for Jennie, who was more trouble than any husband and required more attention than a child. Evelyn didn't know what she would do if Jennie weren't willing to spend her day at St. Hilary's. At first she had thought her mother was getting religion in her dotage, but there didn't seem to be any attempt to proselytize the old people. And then most of them were Catholics already. Maybe they didn't even know that Jennie wasn't one of them.

"Put her in a home," Eddie, her third, said.

"You ever price one of those places?"

"Doesn't she have social security?"

"It takes a lot more than that, Eddie."

Why had she gone on putting up with Jennie when she had had the good sense to get rid of Eddie and her other husbands after they had become nothing but a pain in the neck? Blood is thicker than water? Maybe. But, oh, how Evelyn longed to be free of her mother too.

There was a tapping on the window beside her. Evelyn had to rub the glass with her gloved hand before she could see out. The face of Edna Hospers peered in at her. Evelyn's first thought on looking up into that concerned face was that something had hapened to Jennie. Edna had bad news, that was obvious. Was this how it would happen, on a blustery snowy night in February? Evelyn rolled down the window several inches and snow swirled in at her.

"Could you please come in, Mrs. Cunningham?" Edna's voice was whipped away by the wind.

"What is it?"

"Please. It's your mother."

Evelyn turned off the motor and lights and, assuming

an appropriate expression, pushed open the door. The two women, heads down, shoulders hunched, hurried up the walk to the door of the school.

"Where is she?" Evelyn whispered when they were inside and stamping snow from their feet.

"In the gym. I thought it best to leave her there."

Evelyn looked mournfully at the other woman. "Is that where . . ." She dropped her eyes and felt her lower lip tremble. The thought that something awful had happened to Jennie really did sadden her. She wasn't pretending. This was the beginning of true grief. Tears filled her eyes.

"We can talk in my office."

"But my mother . . ."

"There are others there too. I told her you'd be late tonight. So we could talk."

"You *told* her!"

It took minutes for the confusion to unravel and Evelyn was furious, with Edna and with herself. The fact that she had been so genuinely affected did not diminish the realization that she wanted her mother dead. No! Not dead. She just did not want the responsibility for her anymore. Particularly after Edna started to talk.

"She locked you in a closet? I can't believe that."

"It's true. And there are other things. How old is your mother?"

Evelyn did not have to think. "Seventy-seven."

"She has a beau. Has she told you that?"

"A beau? You mean a man?"

Edna meant a man. Dear God. Listening to the crazy things her mother had been doing, Evelyn found that she believed it all without an effort. Her mother was a nut. She always had been. It was just like her to talk some old duffer into parading around nude in front of the old ladies. Jennie would get a big kick out of that. Why?

"Will you talk to her?" Edna asked.

"Of course I'll talk to her. And she won't ever do anything like this again, I promise you. You must let her continue to come here. I don't know what I'd do if you didn't. I work all day, I don't have time . . ."

On and on. It is the irony of life that the roles of parent and child get reversed like this. Just so her mother had once pleaded on Evelyn's behalf with a school principal after a pajama party that had turned into a nocturnal class meeting. She remembered that her mother had taken her side, had been amused, did not see anything seriously wrong with what she had done. Evelyn half believed now that she had resented her mother's understanding.

Edna said, "Of course she can keep coming. But if she continues to misbehave, well . . ."

"She won't. I promise."

After she had collected her mother and driven home in silence, concentrating on the road only imperfectly visible in the now heavy snowfall, after they had eaten and Jennie had gone to her room to watch television, Evelyn found herself resenting Edna Hospers. How humiliating to have to beg the woman to allow Jennie to come back to that ridiculous place. It was just an old school and there wasn't that much to do. No wonder Jennie tried to liven up the place with a few pranks. They should be grateful to her rather than drag her daughter inside during a snowstorm to discuss Jennie's jokes.

Evelyn made herself a drink, bourbon and 7-up, careful lest Jennie hear and demand one, and snuggled up on the couch in the den with a stack of Frank Sinatra LPs on the machine, prepared to get a little smashed and dreamy. It was her fantasy that, with her dismal marital record, she and Frankie were two of a kind, devil-may-care, foot-loose, fancy-free. Sinatra had lost his mother in a plane crash. The tinkle of ice in her glass, the familiar voice singing with such precision and sureness the familiar words, outside snow falling softly on Fox River—on such a night and in these circumstances she was quite content to be single again. A man would have been an intrusion. Some dreams are best dreamed alone.

Before she turned in, she listened to the late news. What she heard decided her against going to bed just yet. She checked on her mother, who had fallen asleep with the television on, as usual. Evelyn turned the set off, tucked the old woman in, and went into the kitchen where she made another half drink. In the living room she sat sipping it, lights off, staring at the window where snow fell endlessly, and thought of the item on the news.

Enoch Hingle. And they had found his body right where Jennie spent her days, at St. Hilary's. Enoch. Imagine.

8

OUTSIDE, his car was disappearing under the accumulation of snow, but Phil Keegan did not care. He often had the sense of being pleasantly marooned when he spent the evening with Roger Dowling at St. Hilary's rectory. They sat in Roger's book-lined study, the cribbage board on the smoking table between them. As usual, Roger Dowling's pipe went nonstop when they played cards and the room was now dense with smoke.

The priest said, "The truck was stolen and the man already dead when he was driven here?"

"Towed. The gas tank was empty."

Roger Dowling dealt. "Maybe the motor was left running."

"Horvath had the same idea."

"And?"

"The ignition wasn't on."

"How long had the truck been missing?"

Good question. They had put it to Liberati without satisfactory results. Incredibly, the man had retained Tuttle as his counsel.

"You can do better than that," Keegan advised him.

"Watch it, Captain," Tuttle warned.

"I don't see what you want with a lawyer in the first place, Liberati."

"What he doesn't want is a stupid trip down here to have his choice of attorney discussed."

"I remember when lawyers couldn't advertise," Keegan mused.

Liberati, a lean man in his late thirties with an olive complexion, prominent nose, and thick hair already half white, looked at Keegan with lidded eyes.

"You were robbed," Keegan told him.

"I'm missing a truck, yes."

"Missing? Have you missed trucks before?"

"I got the vehicle back. What's the big deal?"

"You got it back? Liberati, we found your damned truck with a dead body in it."

Liberati uncrossed his legs, then crossed them the other way. Cool. Unworried. Well, why should he worry? But then, why had he come accompanied by counsel and, of all possible lawyers, Tuttle? Knowing Tuttle as he did, Keegan could imagine what chicanery might explain this odd combination. Tuttle was not above telling Liberati that he was court appointed to appear with the used-car dealer at police headquarters. Was Liberati that dumb? It is easy to confuse good looks and brains, and vice versa. Few people realized how smart Cy Horvath was, for example, confusing his bigness and that great slab of expressionless face with stupidity. And a lot of people had lived to regret this mistake.

Horvath, with his back to Liberati, asked, "Who looks after your lot nights, Mr. Liberati?"

"What do you mean?" Tuttle barked.

"Liberati?" Horvath turned. "You got a night watchman or what?"

"Owlize. I have a contract with Owlize."

"You have to pay a private firm to guard your property?" Tuttle said, feigning shock. "I remember when a citizen of Fox River could rely on the police department to protect him from thievery."

"So we're agreed the truck was stolen?" Horvath said.

It was the kind of game you could count on with Tuttle on the scene, yet there was no way a man could be denied counsel while he was being questioned. That was about all they did accomplish after half an hour with Liberati, the fact that the truck had indeed been stolen from his lot. He could not say when.

"The snow," he explained. "Business drops to nothing when it snows. The salesmen just sit around in the office keeping warm. No one is out checking the stock."

"If they did, it would have been pretty easy to notice a missing pickup, wouldn't it?" Horvath asked.

"Because of the snow?"

"Yes."

"If someone went out to look. As I said, we sit around in the office . . ."

They took the names of his salesmen, a gesture, routine, but not even Keegan had much faith in his tenet that as often as not it is such tangential information that provides the sought-for explanation.

Keegan lit a cigar when he and Horvath were alone. "Tuttle," he grumbled.

"What's Peanuts been on lately?"

"Why do you ask?"

Horvath shrugged. "Tuttle and Peanuts. It's an old story."

"I still got him in the car with Agnes Lamb."

"Why don't we talk with her?"

Keegan called her in. He had long since learned to follow Cy's hunches. Agnes refused a chair and stood on the opposite side of the desk, erect, chin up.

"At ease," Keegan said.

"Yes, sir." But she did not relax a muscle.

"How do you like working with Pianone, Lamb?"

"I take the assignment I'm given, sir."

Horvath said, "Has he introduced you to Tuttle?"

Her eyes leaped to Cy. "I met Tuttle, yes."

"When?"

But what did they know when they knew that Peanuts had ended his shift the day before at Tuttle's office? As Agnes insisted, the explanation need be no more complicated than the lawyer's offer of a Chinese dinner. Horvath accompanied Agnes from the room and was gone about ten minutes.

"Tuttle called here for Peanuts yesterday," he said when he came back. "That's why they stopped by his office."

Well, if they needed any further incentive to keep an eye on Tuttle, that was certainly it. Keegan decided he would reassign Agnes. He would have liked to assign Peanuts right off the force, but with the political entrenchment of the Pianone family, that was out of the question. Robertson got the sweats whenever Keegan complained to the chief about Peanuts.

"He's a fifth column," Keegan growled. "He doesn't know whose side he's on."

"He has a father and a brother sitting on the City Council, Keegan. We're on his side, and don't forget it."

Telling Roger Dowling these trivia of his day, Keegan marveled at the priest's patience. Why should he be willing to listen to all this junk? Well, thank God he was.

"What have you learned of Enoch Hingle?" Roger asked, putting aside his pipe. That was the signal that the pastor of St. Hilary's had had his fill of cribbage.

"Let me get another beer," Keegan said.

The story on Enoch Hingle was short on facts, yet somehow long in the way the few details they had gathered suggested a significance that had thus far eluded Phil Keegan's ability to articulate. Hingle had grown up on the South Side, parish school, De La Salle High, where his academic record had been undistinguished but where he had shone as an athlete. The *Trib,* the *Sun-Times,* had come up with a dozen photographs of the young Hingle frozen for posterity in the act of releasing a basketball at a hoop, blocking an opponent's shot, driving down the floor. He had been unanimous all-city for two years. And that was it.

"He didn't play in college?"

"He never went to college, Roger. Grades."

"I didn't realize grades were an impediment when a boy has such skill."

"His grades were *really* bad. How he stayed eligible in high school is a mystery."

Roger Dowling's expression indicated he considered that a mystery easily solved. Phil Keegan wondered if the priest could imagine the sequel. After the adulation an athlete receives in high school, after the heady years when the hundreds of thousands of readers of Chicago's major newspapers have read about him as they bounced to their jobs on the RTA, after all that, nothing. It wasn't the fairly ordinary business of an athlete not matching in his subsequent career an earlier promise. Hingle had had no athletic career at all subsequent to the years of teen-age glory. Keegan did not consider it fanciful to believe that for Enoch Hingle his life after the age of eighteen had been anticlimactic, downhill, a bust.

Roger Dowling said, "You said he had run afoul of the law."

"Only once."

"What was the crime?"

Keegan sipped his beer and said as matter-of-factly as he could, "Auto theft."

To his credit, Roger Dowling did not make some dumb remark about a parallel with the stolen pickup. It was hard to resist, of course; Keegan knew. He had fought it in himself, watching Horvath, too, clear it from his mind. That was the kind of irrelevancy that could waste hours of investigation. The thing to notice was that Hingle had been found murdered in a stolen vehicle. There was no certainty he had ever been in the cab of the pickup alive. It made more sense that it had been used as an impromptu hearse to get the body away from where the killing had been done.

"Did he have any connections at all in Fox River?"

Keegan shook his head. There was no need for that link. It was Horvath who had mentioned that someone could have pulled the truck along the Interstate, come off the ramp and parked it where it had been found, and be back on the Interstate within ten minutes.

"Except that the truck was stolen in Fox River," Roger Dowling reminded him.

"Still, the Interstate could have been used."

"And the truck might have been left in any number of places?"

"Do you think that the fact it was abandoned here means anything?"

"It means something to me."

"How so?"

The priest drew on his pipe, but it had gone out. He did not relight it. "I gave him absolution, Phil. You say he was already dead. I wonder if we can be that sure when definitive death comes. I hope it took."

Keegan was vaguely uncomfortable when talk turned to the presuppositions of Roger Dowling's ministry. Not that the captain of detectives believed them any less strongly than the priest. But he felt uncomfortable having certain things said. In his heart, it was easy for him to share Roger's hope that a still-living Enoch Hingle, wanting pardon for his sins, had received absolution of them before appearing before the throne of God.

"I guess he was right-handed at that."

"He needn't have been Catholic, Phil."

"Lucky him."

"That's what I meant," Roger Dowling said.

Driving home through the snow, Phil Keegan was no longer sure he knew what Father Dowling had meant.

9

IGGIE O'BRIEN started Owlize before he left the force. Indeed, it was the prime reason for his leaving when Cleather, Robertson's predecessor, had argued that it was a clear case of conflict of interest for a detective to set up a private security agency.

"You mean I'm competing with the Fox River police? Think about that, chief. If I stop thefts and rip-offs in this town, how am I taking anything away from the police force?"

"You're being paid twice for the same job."

Cleather had been so thin, his enemies had speculated whether it was the crease in his pants rather than bones that held him upright. His enemies had included all but a handful of the Fox River police force. One thing Iggie knew from the outset: once Cleather started fussing about Owlize he was never going to quit. So Iggie quit. He took out his badge and put it on Cleather's desk. He put his weapon beside it.

"Now that I'm a civilian, Cleather, why don't you take that shield and stick it in your ear."

He turned and left the office and for maybe fifteen minutes the elation resulting from telling Cleather to his face what every detective on the force would have liked to tell him buoyed Iggie up. It helped that he was the hero of the squad room. They toasted him with coffee and Coke and just plain water. It was his hour.

"There's only one problem," Phil Keegan said. "You're out of a job. Go back in there and tell him you weren't serious."

"I couldn't do that, Phil."

"Then let me go in and talk to him for you."

"What would you say, that it was an imposter who told him to shove it?"

"I'll tell him you're tired, that you've been working too hard."

"Sure. On two jobs. That's why he called me in."

He would have liked Phil to persist, to drag him in to Cleather and undo the damage, because the truth was that Iggie was frightened to be suddenly out on his own like that. The thing about being a cop was the security it afforded. That sounded nuts, Sally insisted it was, but then, she seemed to think he spent his shift on the wrong end of the pistol range. Still, it was occasionally a dangerous life. But all you had to do was hang in there and survive for twenty years and you had your pension and could go get another job and be paid twice. With seven kids and Sally, Iggie needed the extra money and he had reached a point where he figured he'd get a headstart on the two-job thing. So he founded Owlize. This meant he had some stationery printed, selected a motto—Owlize Gives A Hoot—, got incorporated for twenty-five bucks—Tuttle even let him pay that off in installments, with interest, of course— got some magnetic plastic signs to stick on the front doors of the family station wagon, and went about signing up customers.

That was the theory. Go out and talk to businesses about this new service. A flying squad of watchmen, making regular checks throughout the night, supplementing police surveillance. Iggie didn't do very well until he mentioned a few facts about the extent of police coverage during the night. It wasn't a professional secret that from midnight to eight in the morning there were only four patrol cars on duty in the whole of Fox River. The city was divided into quadrants, each car had responsibility for a fourth of the city, and that was it. When you added to this the fact that those cars didn't spend the night endlessly patrolling the streets, the small businessman began to look a bit worried. That wasn't his idea of protection.

Don't knock the police, Iggie would tell them. It's a question of taxes. Indignation would die down with that, and Iggie learned how to move into the receptive outlook he had created. Within a month he had his oldest boy Martin at work in the first Owlize patrol car, a VW Bug painted black and white with a flasher mounted on the roof. The prospect of putting all five of his sons in Owlize patrol cars stirred a dynastic streak in Iggie's soul he had not realized was there. In his mind's eye he began to see whole battalions of employees, fleets of cars cruising the city during the night hours, protecting the property of his prudent clients.

So old Cleather had struck a nerve when he said Iggie was competing with the Fox River police force. He *had* dreamed that dream, and of course that was the trouble. It was only in his imagination and hopes that Owlize was a thriving business. In the weeks after his resignation, Sally spent a lot of time alone in their darkened bedroom with a damp washcloth on her eyes and forehead. A sick headache, she called it, but it was clear to Iggie who her headache was and what she was sick of. When he showed her the stationery and her name on the letterhead as vice-president, she burst into tears, and they weren't tears of joy. Iggie resolved that he would show her. He would show Cleather too. He would show the whole damned world. And wasn't Owlize a perfect name for his undertaking?

"Undertaking?" Phil Keegan said. "I thought you said night watchman."

"You know what I mean, Phil."

"I know I think you're nuts. You need any money to tide you over?"

"Thanks for the offer."

"You turning it down?"

"For the present. Tuttle says I can owe him."

"A piece of advice, Iggie. Never owe Tuttle anything."

Iggie didn't intend to owe anybody anything, not if he could help it. But how could you dislike a guy who put his deceased father's name into the title of his law firm? Tuttle & Tuttle. The senior Tuttle had been a fireman on the railroad but he was immortalized on his son's door because he had put him through law school. Besides, Tuttle was the cheapest lawyer in town. And he had thought making Sally vice-president was a nice touch. That was when he told Iggie about his father.

Owlize had prospered. Now Iggie's son Martin was in law school, but Stevie and Jack were working for their father. They wore uniforms and Stevie took his German shepherd with him on his nightly rounds. Jack, six foot four and looking bigger in the VW, was formidable enough without a dog. Anyway, Pluto, the German shepherd, was about as ferocious as a goldfish. Liberati's lot was on Stevie's run, and when Iggie heard about the stolen pickup he was mad as hell.

Stevie got mad too. "When did he report it?" he wanted to know. "And how do we know it happened at night?"

Good questions, both of them. Liberati hadn't reported

the theft. It was Tuttle who came by with the story, bringing Peanuts with him.

"I already talked with him, Iggie. He has decided not to sue you."

"Did you recommend that he should?"

"It's all impersonal," Tuttle said with a wave of his hand. "You're insured, aren't you?"

"And the insurance company's money isn't real? They collect it from guys like me, Tuttle. If Liberati does sue me, I'll break your head."

Peanuts stirred and Tuttle put a hand on the policeman's arm. "I told you. He isn't going to sue. I think he's making a mistake, but it's his decision. If he had decided to sue, Iggie, we would have worked something out."

Iggie knew enough to know that he did not want to hear just what arrangemets Tuttle had had in mind. He really ought to get rid of Tuttle. The little lawyer had been legal counsel for Owlize from the beginning, he was still comparatively cheap, and, as long as Iggie didn't take any of the shady advice Tuttle kept coming up with, everything was okay. Maybe he didn't need a lawyer anyway. In a couple of years, after Martin finished law school, he would become his son's client. The thou he paid Tuttle as an annual retainer could stay in the family. Meanwhile he would leave things as they were. After all, if it hadn't been for Tuttle, how would he have learned of Liberati's stolen truck?

"It had a body in it," Peanuts said, snapping his gum.

"When they found it," Tuttle explained. "Some guy shot full of holes. The truck was parked by Saint Hilary's rectory."

Tuttle recited these facts without expression. His attention was engaged only when he saw some opportunity for exploitation, and the body found in the stolen truck apparently did not qualify. Iggie got rid of Tuttle and Peanuts. He wanted to go wake up Stevie and tell him what had happened to a client Stevie was responsible for. And Stevie got the ball right back into his father's court. Why hadn't Liberati complained? And how did they know the theft had occurred when Owlize was responsible for the Liberati lot? Iggie decided to go over and talk with his client.

Stevie said, "You want me to come along?"

"If you can be out of that bed and ready to go in twenty minutes."

Stevie made it in fifteen and Iggie found himself admiring the boy. Stevie was no happier than his father that Liberati had been ripped off.

Both of them were unhappier still when they had to sit around at Liberati's, waiting for their client to see them. Liberati worked out of a mobile home mounted on cinder blocks. Inside, there was only one division, that between Liberati's office and the rest of the place. So Iggie and Stevie sat there with the snow melting from their shoes onto the indoor-outdoor carpeting, listening to the three salesmen shoot the breeze. They didn't look too disappointed that the weather kept customers away. For that matter, Iggie wondered why Liberati would need three salesmen on a sunny day. Three salesmen plus the secretary.

It was the secretary who made Iggie anxious to get in there and talk to Liberati and get the hell out. Iggie didn't like the way the girl looked at Stevie and he liked even less the way his son looked at the girl. The way she traded good-natured insults with the poker-playing salesmen, the depth of her neckline, and the brassy look in her eyes, suggested to Iggie that she had been around. Charmaine. That was her name. The salesmen called her Chow Mein. She shrugged her shoulders expressively, with noticeable effect on her massive breasts, and looked with sultry eyes at Stevie for commiseration.

"Those fellas are stir crazy from all this snow."

"Cabin fever, Chow Mein. I caught it from you."

Iggie actually blushed at the roar of suggestive laughter. Charmaine joined in. Honest to God, what ever happened to female modesty? If Sally knew Stevie was exposed to this sort of thing, she would hit the roof.

"Tell Mr. Liberati I don't have all day, will you, Miss?"

"He knows you're here, Mr. O'Brien."

"Say, O'Brien," one of the salesmen said, "weren't you once a cop?" He made it sound like a crime.

"Why do you ask?"

"No reason." This guy was hollow-cheeked and Iggie would bet pigeon-breasted as well, but he had a heavy beard that made him look tough anyway. Iggie could half believe he had met him before, in the line of duty.

"What's your name?"

For answer, the man turned the plastic nameplate on his desk toward Iggie. J. J. Green. Iggie got up, lit a cigarette, and walked to the door where he looked out at the snow. When he turned, he glanced at the nameplates on the other desks. P. L. Black. Jack White. Black, White, and Green? They sounded like a color chart. Iggie wondered why he hadn't noticed that before. Those names were as phony as this long delay. Why the hell was Liberati so busy that he couldn't see the man he paid to protect his property, particularly after a truck had been stolen from his lot?

10

ROGER DOWLING had long thoughts about Enoch Hingle after Phil Keegan left the rectory. Unlike the detective, the priest did not see Hingle only as a man who had lost a chance to go on doing what he already did well, to do it before larger audiences, perhaps to make a living at it. No doubt that must have been an attractive prospect for the young man. But Roger Dowling thought too of the parish school the boy had attended and then the Catholic high school. Had they prepared him to see his life in terms other than the possibility of becoming a celebrity, a success in the obvious and worldly sense?

But then, who would have thought the boy would have had to learn so soon that we cannot put our trust in the things of this world? He would have been taught that, in one sense, by way of the catechism at least. Enoch Hingle was old enough to have been taught in the traditional way. That meant memoriz ing successive versions of the Baltimore Catechism, a method unfairly maligned, in Roger Dowling's estimation. Of course, learning answers by rote did not automatically make one a good Catholic or good anything else. No one had ever imagined it did. But the young had acquired the lore of their faith, furniture for their minds, definitions they would carry with them till the day they died. Roger Dowling would wager that Enoch Hingle would have been able to rattle off the names of the seven sacraments, the definition of mortal sin, perhaps even the Gifts of the Holy Ghost. More pertinently, he would have known the requirements for a perfect act of contrition. Father Dowling hoped Hingle had not only remembered what such a prayer was, but had said it before his life was so cruelly snuffed out.

For some reason, Roger Dowling always thought of Lee Harvey Oswald when he heard of a man being shot. Oswald, caught forever in the famous photograph, hand clutched to his body, the expression on his face one of incredulity, the rejection of the possibility that this could be happening to *him,* the bullet actually entering *his* body, invading *him,* claiming *his* life. However guilty Oswald was of inflicting the same thing on President Kennedy and John Connolly, there was a shock of disbelief at seeing it, and like most of the nation, Roger Dowling had watched this killing on the television screen. Enoch Hingle had had a whole clip of .22 shells pumped into his body. Father Dowling shook his head. Where was the body now?

He thought too of the surviving family of the victim. If there were any survivors. A call to Phil Keegan brought the information that the body had been claimed and transported to Mooney Brothers on the South Side. Father Dowling gave them a call and, after a succession of mournful voices, was put through to F. X. Mooney himself.

"F. X. Mooney," the senior partner said in sepulchral tones.

"This is Father Dowling of Saint Hilary's parish in Fox River, Mr. Mooney. I understand that the body of Enoch Hingle has been taken to your establishment."

"That's right, Father."

"The body was found in the street outside my rectory."

"I see."

Father Dowling could imagine Mooney sit forward and frown at the apparent suggestion that Mooney Brothers were poaching on his territory.

"I understand that the family claimed the body."

"His sister." Mooney's voice was now distant and cold.

"Is her name Hingle still?"

"What parish did you say you are in, Father?"

"Saint Hilary's. In Fox River. I would like to get in touch with the family."

"Saint Raphael's, which is Mrs. Ludwig's parish, is taking care of matters, Father. Perhaps you should contact them."

"Good idea. And thank you. You've been very helpful."

Roger Dowling consulted the Archdiocesan Directory and discovered that the pastor of St. Raphael's was one Thomas Lothian. Lothian? Lothian? The name did not ring a bell. There were three assistants at St. Raphael's and the name Doremus did ring a bell. There had been a Doremus just a few years behind Roger Dowling at Mundelein. Charles Doremus. And he had come several times to sessions of the Archdiocesan Marriage Court when Roger Dowling sat on that tribunal. Roger Dowling's memory of Doremus was of a small wispy man whose thin hair seemed always in the grip of static electricity. A diffident man. A kind man. Like Roger Dowling himself, Doremus had permitted his emotions to get tangled up in the case of a plaintiff before the court.

Roger Dowling dialed the rectory of St. Raphael's and

asked for Father Doremus. He was not in. Was he expected soon? Who is calling, please? When he had identified himself as a priest, cordiality returned to the housekeeper's voice. Father was expected within the hour and she would have Father return Father's call. Roger Dowling thanked her and put down the phone.

Marie Murkin had been pushing a dust mop back and forth in the hall outside the pastor's study while he made these phone calls.

"What was that all about?" she asked over her shoulder, working the mop back and forth now just outside the door.

"All what, Marie?"

She hummed a bit, turned, glanced around the study without meeting his eye. She shook her head as if overwhelmed with the messiness of the room. It was off limits to her cleaning zeal; she was forbidden to put what she considered to be order into Roger Dowling's study. He wanted things just the way they were. Mrs. Murkin could unleash her animus against dust and disorder anywhere else in the house.

"Are you planning to concelebrate the funeral Mass?"

Marie Murkin knew his views about concelebration and doubtless counted on reference to it to sting him into loquacity.

"We have no funeral Masses scheduled, Marie."

She made an impatient noise. "Father, I heard you talking about that poor Hingle. And I couldn't help it. I was cleaning the hallway and you left your door open."

The ringing telephone saved Roger Dowling from replying. When he said Hello, Marie followed her mop into the hallway but Roger Dowling was sure she was well within earshot. He really didn't mind. And he was ashamed of himself for teasing her like that. His caller was Charles Doremus.

"I don't know if you remember me, Father Doremus, but—"

"Of course I remember you. What are you doing at Saint Hilary's in Fox River?"

"I am pastor here."

"You're no longer on the marriage court?"

There was a lesson of sorts in Doremus's question. How easily we think that the events in our life are played before a world audience, that no triuimph or disgrace of ours can fail to be known to everyone. Roger Dowling's fall from grace had seemed to him as dramatic as the fall of Lucifer, streaking earthward through the ecclesiastical skies. Surely all his brother priests would know of his removal to the sanitarium in Wisconsin and his further remove to St. Hilary's in Fox River. Even now, long after he had come to see St. Hilary's as the best thing that had ever happened to him, he could recall the shame with which he had assumed his parish. He told Doremus he was no longer on the marriage court.

"What a relief that must be."

"Yes, Father, it is. Do you know anything about Enoch Hingle?"

"One of your cases?"

"No, this is a man whose body was found just outside my rectory, in a truck, a few nights ago. His sister lives in Saint Raphael's."

"His *body* was found?"

"He had been killed. Shot."

There was a gasp at the other end of the line. "Dear God in heaven."

"His sister is called Mrs. Ludwig."

"It was her brother who was killed?"

"That's right."

"Ludwig. I don't know her. Good heavens, this is awful. What is it you wanted, Father?"

"I had hoped you might know Mrs. Ludwig. Who will be saying the funeral Mass?"

"I don't know. I'll ask."

The phone was put down and Roger Dowling waited. He half regretted disturbing Father Doremus with this alarming news and he wondered if his desire to talk with Mrs. Ludwig could withstand scrutiny. She was a Catholic and bereaved. He was a priest. He had a special obligation to comfort the sorrowful. But he could not deceive himself that his chief motive was curiosity about her dead brother.

"Father Dowling?" It was Father Doremus returned. "Yes?"

"An incredible thing. I've been assigned the Hingle funeral. That is the name of the deceased. Hingle."

"I know."

"The thought of talking to someone whose brother has been shot, well, I just don't know. Not that I'm surprised I got the assignment." A dull edge got into Doremus's tremulous voice.

"I'd be happy to take the funeral for you, Father. Because of my connection with the deceased."

"Do you mean it?"

"Of course. If Father Lothian approves, that is."

"Monsignor Lothian. He'll approve. He won't care." Doremus paused. "He's in Florida."

Who made the assignments, the housekeeper? Doremus was first assistant and should be in charge when the pastor was away. In any case, no obstacle stood in the way of Roger Dowling taking over for Doremus. This would entail leading the rosary tonight at Mooney's, saying the funeral Mass in the morning, and going on to the cemetery for the burial.

"Would you have a spare room there, Father?"

"Certainly, Father Dowling. By all means."

"That is very kind of you."

"Not at all. Not at all." Doremus was almost cheerful now. No wonder he was still an assistant.

Before hanging up, Roger Dowling asked for and got Mrs. Ludwig's telephone number and address. He thought he might stop by her house on his way to St. Raphael's.

In the hallway Marie Murkin coughed in an unconvincing way. Father Dowling filled his pipe, lit it, and puffed silently for a minute. He became aware of Mrs. Murkin standing in the doorway of the study.

"I'll be staying in Chicago tonight, Marie. At Saint Raphael's parish. I'll leave the number for you. I should be back by tomorrow noon."

"In time for Mass?"

"I'll be saying Mass at Saint Raphael's."

"Whatever for?"

"A funeral Mass, Marie. For Enoch Hingle."

"I thought that's what it was," Marie Murkin said, taking the edges of her apron as if she meant to curtsy. There was a smile on her face when she turned away from him. But she did not leave the room.

"Who will say Mass here tomorrow, Father?"

"Charles Doremus. You'll like him. A very fine priest."

"Where's he from?"

"Saint Raphael's."

Marie nodded contentedly as her universe resumed a rational look. Her humming as she went back to the kitchen was a genuine sign of relief. She hated not to know exactly what was going on. Well, who doesn't?

11

HORVATH parked his car across the street and waited while O'Brien and his son were inside talking to Liberati. Owlize filed a list of its clients with the police and Horvath had run through it and, sure enough, there was Liberati's name. He did not know why he had consulted the list or why it seemed important that the used-car dealer's name was on it, but he left headquarters with the hunch that he might be on to something.

He said nothing to Captain Keegan. If he kept checking everything with Keegan, Keegan would get himself another assistant. Horvath knew he was supposed to use his own head, take the initiative, tell Keegan things he didn't already know. With Iggie O'Brien in the picture, there was another reason.

Horvath knew how much Keegan liked Iggie O'Brien. That in itself was a surprise because normally Keegan had nothing to do with former members of the force, even those who had put in their years and taken their pensions. Keegan seemed to think it a mark of disloyalty for a man to take retirement after only twenty years' active duty. The truth was that Horvath half agreed with Keegan. But Iggie O'Brien was an exception, at least for Keegan.

They were always bad, exceptions like that, as Keegan would have been the first to point out. Cy Horvath doubted very much that Phil Keegan had had the thought that occurred to him. It could have been an inside job, the theft of that pickup, or the next thing to an inside job. That's when he thought of Owlize and decided to check its list. It wouldn't be a new thing, the man hired to protect property being tempted by the thought that he could steal with impunity. Just as there were cops who were introduced to the seamy side of life in the line of duty and were drawn fatally into a moral underworld. Rookies had to be watched. It sometimes happened that one crew of cops found themselves watching another crew off duty, hanging around honky-tonk bars, looking for trouble and usually finding it. Horvath thought it might be a good idea to find out if Iggie O'Brien or his son Stephen had succumbed to a similar temptation. If one or the other was connected with the theft of the pickup, they were thereby connected with the death of Enoch Hingle.

The fact that Iggie and his son had been in the mobile home Liberati used for an office for over an hour caused Horvath to think his hunch was a good one. Another fifteen minutes went by and then the door opened. But it was not the O'Briens who came out. Horvath had tipped the rearview mirror so he could watch the door of Liberati's office without looking at it. The man who stood in the doorway lighting a cigarette made Horvath drop all caution. He turned and stared at the man. There was no doubt who he was.

Horvath was out of the car and moving on the run toward Joe DiNigro in one fluid motion.

DiNigro was waving out a match and exhaling smoke when he saw Horvath coming at him. A second of doubt and then he flicked his cigarette at the oncoming Horvath, dropped to his knee as his hand disappeared inside his jacket. Horvath had cleared his weapon as he ran and he brought it up now, steadying it with his left hand.

"Don't try, Dinnie."

Dinnie tried. Horvath's shot caught DiNigro in the arm. He cried out, his weapon spun free, and he crashed back into the door. Horvath scooped up DiNigro's gun and stood over the wounded hoodlum.

"I told you not to try."

DiNigro, wincing with pain, sputtered an obscenity. The door behind him opened and Iggie O'Brien came out.

"Horvath! What the hell happened?"

Horvath, looking at Iggie, wondered if his hunch really had anything to do with Owlize. But DiNigro's presence suggested that the theory of an inside job might be true.

"Who's inside?" Horvath asked.

Liberati looked out over O'Brien's shoulder and his dark eyes sparked with anger. Horvath was not its object. Pushing past Iggie, Liberati grabbed DiNigro by his good arm.

"Were you carrying a piece, you stupid ass? You're fired. Get the hell out of here."

"He isn't going anywhere without me, Liberati," Horvath said. "Let's all of us go inside."

Inside it was like old home week. Albini and Gruening were like filling an inside straight. Liberati professed to be astonished to learn that all these men were wanted for questioning on a variety of counts. Horvath neither believed nor disbelieved him. All he knew was that any cop in the country would recognize this trio from the constant circulation of their photographs.

"They're salesmen," Liberati insisted. "They had recommendations."

"You hired them all at once?"

Liberati decided he didn't want to talk about it until he consulted his lawyer. Tuttle? Ye gods. Horvath put in a call to Keegan. Whatever the hell was going on here, Keegan would want to be in on it from the start. And he wasn't going to like it that Iggie O'Brien had gotten mixed up with a bunch like this.

Keegan said to keep everyone right there. He would be there in minutes.

And he was.

The session in Liberati's office was long, interesting, and inconclusive. The fact that Liberati had hired as salesmen three convicted felons, two of whom were currently the object of a police search, could hardly be dismissed as an accident, though that is what Liberati expected them to do.

"How am I supposed to know they're crooks, Keegan? Have I got some duty to run a check on everybody I hire?"

"You hired them all the same day?"

"I just opened the lot. I'm hiring. These guys answer my ad. They got credentials, letters, I hire them."

"What ad?"

Liberati paused to light a filter-tipped cigarette that he inspected carefully before putting into his mouth. "I don't mean ad. They must have seen the announcement in the paper about the opening of the lot. They came here and we talked and I thought, here's a good deal, a whole crew at once, so I took them on." Liberati's face glowed with sudden anger. "And this bum is walking around my lot carrying a gun." He drew back his hand to take a swing at DiNigro but Horvath stopped him. It did not take much effort. Like his story, Liberati's anger seemed phony to Cy Horvath.

"How about your stock?" Horvath asked. "Did you pick that up all at once too?"

"Most of it came from a wholesaler, sure." Liberati turned to blow smoke away from Horvath, then studied the lieutenant. "Look, you got a legitimate complaint against Di-Nigro. Against Gruening too. Okay. But I don't like the insinuation like maybe Liberati did something wrong."

"Wrong things just happen to you," Keegan said. "First, one of your trucks is stolen and when it is found there is a dead body in it. Now it turns out that your whole sales crew is made up of hoodlums. To top it all off, you've got Tuttle for a lawyer."

The last remark was prompted by the arrival of the little lawyer. His car swung in from the street and sped across the lot and then went into a swerve as he put on the brakes. Horvath, standing at the door, looked out at the car and was sure it was going to slide right into the mobile home, but somehow Tuttle managed to swing the wheel, correct his slide, and come to a jarring stop by colliding with the rear end of a four-wheel drive truck whose center of gravity was a foot higher than the roof of Tuttle's car. Tuttle popped from the car as if from the force of its impact with the truck and came on the run toward the office. Horvath opened the door for him, surprising Tuttle, who hesitated a moment, then ducked into the office. He stood stamping snow from his feet and glaring from under the brim of his Irish tweed hat at Keegan and Liberati and the seated sales crew.

"Hello, Mr. Tuttle," the secretary sang out. She had offered to make coffee and now smiled at Tuttle through the steam rising from the mugs she carried.

"Are you too being detained against your will, Charmaine?" Tuttle asked sternly.

"I work here, Mr. Tuttle."

Tuttle ignored her and tried to ignore Keegan too as he addressed Liberati. "Liberati, you would be perfectly within your rights if you ordered these men out of here. If they care to come back with a warrant—"

"Shut up, Tuttle," Keegan advised.

Horvath walked toward the little lawyer with a chair, placed it behind him, and urged him into a seated position. "We are speaking with three convicted felons, two of whom are wanted in various parts of the country. Are you representing them, Tuttle?"

"I may. I may. That all depends."

"You don't represent them, Tuttle," Liberati told him.

"I am here in answer to your call," Tuttle said plaintively.

"That S.O.B. DiNigro pulled a gun on Horvath. That's why he's bleeding."

Tuttle half rose from his chair and looked at the blood-reddened towel DiNigro had wrapped around his arm. The lawyer turned pale. "Do you mean he's been shot? That man must see a doctor!"

"I took care of it, Mr. Tuttle," Charmaine said, handing the lawyer a mug of steaming coffee. He looked as if he needed it more than the others.

"Thank you, Charmaine." Tuttle dipped toward the mug and began to inhale the scalding coffee.

The most disconsolate-looking man in the room, Horvath decided, was Iggie O'Brien. He had slumped into a desk chair, crossed his arms and legs, and sat silently through the wait for Keegan and then the interrogation that had gone around in circles. O'Brien's kid kept his eye on Charmaine, which, Horvath conceded, was pretty hard not to do. She was what might be called a full-blown girl. Woman, not girl. Charmaine would never see the sunny side of thirty again.

After an hour of fencing with the three salesmen and Liberati, Keegan decided there was no alternative to getting tough. He announced they were all under arrest. Tuttle hit the fan, spilling half of his third mug of coffee as he did so.

"What's the charge, Keegan?"

"Suspicion of murder."

That brought Liberati to his feet. DiNigro had not even used his gun, let alone shot and killed anybody.

"He's the one got shot, Keegan. He could maybe sue Horvath."

"I'm talking of the death of Enoch Hingle," Keegan said. "Cy, phone for the wagon."

Tuttle and Liberati huddled, the lawyer throwing glances over one shoulder at the three salesmen who continued to sit impassively. Tuttle might have been a sandlot quarterback surveying the opponent's defensive setup. Or he might have been what he was, a lawyer advising his client to separate himself as quickly and clearly as possible from his sales force.

"Keegan," Tuttle said, sidling up to where Horvath and the captain of detectives were looking out at the lot where more snow drifted down and transformed Liberati's stock into fluffy formless objects. "Keegan, let's cut Liberati out of this deal. You know he had nothing to do with that killing."

"How do I know that, Tuttle?"

"He's just a small businessman. He's a native of this town. I've known him for years. You've known him for years."

This was true enough of Horvath, if not of Keegan. Cy could remember from the time he was a kid, going over to the marina that Liberati's parents had run on the Fox River. There was mooring for powerboats and sailboats and canoes for rental. In high school it had been the place to take your girl on a summer weekend. Liberati inherited the marina from his parents and, as far as Horvath knew, still operated it. The used-car lot was apparently a winter job, a way to bring in some money during the months when the marina was shut down. Keegan must know all this too, as Tuttle suggested, but he merely shook his head.

"He's coming along, Tuttle. And so are you."

"You're kidding."

"Don't bet on it."

The wagon came and Liberati, Tuttle, and the three salesmen went out the door. When he separated from the others to head for his car, Tuttle walked as if he expected to be collared and hustled into the wagon with the other miscreants.

"How the hell did you get mixed up with this bunch, Iggie?" Keegan asked.

Iggie shook his head woefully. "I came over here to talk to Liberati. He's a client. I wanted to know why he didn't raise hell with me after a truck was stolen off his lot."

"What was the answer?"

"I didn't get to put the question. I didn't even get in to talk to him. He stalled me. Stevie and I were sitting here cooling our heels when Horvath and Black—DiNigro—had the little encounter outside."

Stevie was in the back of the office talking with Charmaine. Keegan frowned at the scene, much as Iggie himself did. "Take Stevie and get the hell out of here, O'Brien."

"I still want to know, Phil."

"Know what?"

"Why Liberati didn't complain."

"So do I, Iggie. So do I."

12

MARCUS RIEHLE said his night prayers kneeling on the floor beside his bed. He asked God to take care of his parents who had died, and all his friends and acquaintances. The latter categories were left anonymous. Marcus Riehle did not want to bother God with the fact that he had no friends and few acquaintances. Finally, as the bishop who had given the commencement address when Riehle graduated from high school had advised the class to do, Riehle singled out his enemies and especially commended them to God's mercy. To the name of Mrs. Ennis he now added the name of the security man at the public library who had hustled him so ignominiously into the night a week before.

Riehle never asked favors for himself. He did, in general terms, thank God for all graces and favors he had received, but he had no menu of items he wanted for himself. The truth was that he was so overwhelmed by the success he enjoyed as a writer, and had enjoyed ever since he turned to the writing of pamphlets, that he superstitiously avoided making explicit mention of it lest God realize that He had meant that success for a more deserving person than Marcus Riehle.

"God bless Mrs. Ennis," he prayed.

Why did he consider her his enemy? She would not know him if she saw him. His name would ring no bell for her. It was childish to resent the authority with which she invited the city's authors to gather around her at the public library every fortnight as if she were their patroness, their muse, their preceptor. Yet he did resent her, deeply. So far as he knew, she had had no success as an author. So far as he knew, she had not even known an author's failure. Had she written and not found a publisher for her writings? It was likely, but he had no certainty in the matter.

The reason for his hatred was presumptive, anticipatory: he assumed that if she did know who he was, she would despise him as a mere pamphleteer. She who, for all the world knew, had written nothing more literary than a check, would look down on him as a hack who wrote religious pamphlets, the implication being that this was something she could do, that anyone could do, if they chose to lower themselves to that level.

Not that Mrs. Ennis was disdainful of religion, an agnostic, a Sunday-morning slugabed. On the contrary. She was an adornment of the St. Hilary choir loft at the ten-thirty Mass on Sunday morning, the Mass sung by the angelic-voiced Franciscan who helped Father Dowling on weekends. Marcus Riehle was of course an habitué of that same Mass. He came late, prowled about among the pamphlets for a time, permitting his eye to drop as if by chance on one or another title of his own. And then, when the ushers were once more convinced he did not want to be led down the aisle to an empty pew, Riehle climbed the curling stairway that led to the choir loft and, at the top, on a triangular landing, stood staring in at the choir and Mrs. Ennis.

Among the faults he repeatedly confessed was inattention at Mass. And at prayer. His knees were numb, he still knelt beside his bed, but his thought had drifted far from his prayers. He crossed himself hastily and slipped into bed, lying on his back, pulling the covers to his chin and staring at the ceiling where light flickered in an odd way. He fancied himself a drowned man, lying at the bottom of a lake, staring up through the cold depths at the surface on which the daytime sun softly played. He closed his eyes and saw Mrs. Ennis.

She was a widow. He did not lust after another man's wife. It would have been an exaggeration to say that he lusted after the maritally unencumbered Mrs. Ennis. Marcus Riehle, except for a shameless weekend at a Mexican border town when he first got out of bootcamp, had very little knowledge of what went on between man and woman when the lights were off and they were in bed together. He threw back the covers, finding them suddenly stifling. He breathed a little prayer, asking that his heart be pure and his mind free of sinful thoughts.

If in his imagination Mrs. Ennis looked down upon his literary achievements, he could not bear to think what she would say to any amorous importuning on his part. Quite aside from his unprepossessing manner, there was his damnable stammer. He could not even tell her what was in his heart.

It was odd that he did not stutter in his dreams. In his dreams, he had approached Mrs. Ennis and fluently expressed his admiration for the sterling job she was doing with the Fox River writers club. He knew a thing or two about organization, he could imagine the difficulties one faced in getting people to come out to a meeting at night, no matter the intrinsic interest of the topic to be discussed, no matter the appeal to their self-interest. Where, after all, could they go for better—and free!—advice on their writing aspirations than to Mrs. Ennis? In his dreams he had approached her, she had responded to his overture, and this introduced a new element into their relationship. He had relentlessly pursued, taking advantage of her maidenly confusion. They had known sexual congress. Afterward, half faint in his arms, Mrs. Ennis confessed that for months she had admired him from afar.

Marcus Riehle awoke to a world where he stuttered and where Mrs. Ennis did not know he existed and where he was perspiring freely in a room in which the thermostat had been lowered to 65 for the night. Awake, he tried to imagine their wedding, his and Mrs. Ennis's. He thought of her singing at the wedding, though she herself was the bride. He imagined them hurrying down the aisle afterward, between pews of happy well-wishing friends. He tried, but he could not dream while he was awake.

He hated Mrs. Ennis.

On the ceiling, lights shifted, furry and soft, indistinct, messages sent from traffic near and far, filtered, refracted, finally flickering there above his bed, the surface of the sea. He did not count sheep; he counted pamphlets. During the past week he had written three new ones. *How To Change Your Life* was one of them. How facile it was to lay out plans for others to follow. Riehle wrote, as always, with complete sincerity. While the words formed themselves as if by magic on the page before him, popping from the dancing ball of his selectric typewriter onto the yellow pages he used for drafts, he really believed that the twelve steps he enumerated and then developed were precisely the dozen necessary to alter one's whole life. He was his own best reader. Even as he wrote the advice, he could imagine himself keeping a small notebook always on hand in which to record the triumphs and defeats of his day. "Double-entry moral bookkeeping" he dubbed it, best kept in a code, several examples of which were to be found in the appendix of the pamphlet. Riehle had always been fascinated by codes.

As soon as that pamphlet was finished, he was finished with it, turning immediately to *God's Judgment on Russia*. This topic had suggested itself when he skimmed through the volumes of Solzhenitsyn's *Gulag Archipelago*. The divine judgment on Russia was harsh but, lest his reader be tempted by chauvinist pride, Riehle, again echoing Solzhenitsyn, added that the divine judgment on the West might be even more severe than that on Mother Russia. Finally, just today, Marcus Riehle had written *A Great Mystery*.

The subject was marriage, the contents culled from his assiduous reading of somewhat sedate religious marriage manuals, but the real significance of the pamphlet was its dedication. To M.E. The initials stood for Martha Ennis. Recalling that dedication now, Marcus Riehle was filled with a rare excitement. It was a coded declaration of his feeling for her, as obscure as the letter he had sent her pseudonymously. How could she ever know?

He squeezed his eyes shut and in the resultant fireworks murmured a wordless prayer to God. His relation to Martha Ennis was triadic, via the Divinity. If it was true, as he believed it was, that all humans are connected because of their destiny to exist forever with God, it was not fanciful for him to think of God as his true link with Martha Ennis. This made it real, more than a mere hope; it was already achieved. All that remained was for her to recognize it.

A Great Mystery, with its dedication, would stir her curiosity. She would look again at the cover. Marcus Riehle. Perhaps she would then study the rack at the back of St. Hilary's and see how many pamphlets he had written. Mere pamphlets? But there was one dedicated to M.E. How could she regard that as insignificant? She could not. She would search him out and that would make all the difference in the world. He could always deny that M.E. stood for Martha Ennis. "My dear lady, I do not even know you. Why on earth would I dedicate a pamphlet to you?" So he was covered. And what if she should ask who M.E. was? The answer that occurred to him opened his eyes. Lights still moved ectoplasmically on the ceiling overhead. To ME. *Ad meipsum.* A letter to myself. The circle of egocentricity. Marcus Riehle dedicates pamphlet on marriage to Marcus Riehle.

Staring at the ceiling, naked to his God if not to his enemies, Marcus Riehle saw that he was a ridiculous figure. But what did it matter? Who besides himself was disappointed in him? God? But perhaps God is disappointed in all of us. That is a truth not all of us realize, he added grimly to God and to himself. And then, remembering, he hopped out of bed and knelt once more.

"And God bless Marie Murkin," Marcus Riehle prayed.

13

PHIL KEEGAN sat at the kitchen table of his apartment with a cup of cold coffee before him—behind him, one light on in the living room—staring at the glass doors that gave onto the balcony. Now at night the glass played back to him the image of his apartment. Reflected like that, the place looked almost cozy. He was not included in the picture, not at this angle; all he saw was an empty living room. He lit a cigarette and exhaled smoke angrily. What the hell was going on?

He would have preferred rehearsing his confusion aloud with Roger Dowling, but the priest was busy tonight and Keegan was thrown back on his own resources. It made him realize how much of a habit it had become for him to stop at St. Hilary's rectory, at noon for lunch after midday Mass, at night for beer and cribbage and, in season, the Cubs on radio or the tube.

Sometimes he was there twice in the same day. Was he making a pest of himself? It was difficult to think so. Quite apart from the welcome he invariably received from Roger, there was the attitude of Marie Murkin. Keegan was sure she would have tipped her hand if either the pastor or she found Keegan too frequent a presence. Maybe he wasn't a good judge, however, since he had come to depend so much on those visits.

Several times he had actually thought of suggesting to Roger that they invest in a retirement condominium together. Somewhere in Florida, maybe, or Arizona. Someplace pleasant and warm and far from Fox River. Imagine the two of them living out their days lying in the sun or trying to catch some fish.

It would never happen. Phil Keegan, at his personal half-century mark, knew there were a lot of things that would never happen. It was far better for him to take his life as it was and realize that this is how it was going to be, right to the end. There were a lot worse things than that. It was a good job, captain of detectives. If Robertson weren't such an ass, it would be a great job. But Robertson was an ass. It was never more evident than at a time like this, when neither Keegan nor Horvath could figure out what was going on. Sure as shooting that is when Robertson would want a little chat with Keegan in the chief's office. When Robertson came to Keegan's office it was a sign not only that things were going well but that even the chief knew they were. Robertson was a creature of the political clique that included the Pianones. Like it or not, Robertson was a fixture, part of the life Keegan was destined to live until there was no life left.

"What's this about Liberati, Phil?"

"Good question. A murdered man was found in a truck stolen from his lot and now we find he had three men with records employed as salesmen."

Robertson frowned. "How many convictions?"

"So far? Two apiece. It will probably be three for Di-Nigro and Gruening."

"A charge of harassment has been filed, Captain."

"Tuttle." Keegan sneered.

"Any charge brought against the force is serious."

"Chief, one of those bastards pulled a gun on Horvath."

Robertson pinched the end of his nose between thumb and forefinger. "I refer to Mr. Liberati. Why was he brought down here in the wagon with the rest of them?"

"For questioning. I had him in the other day too."

"Did you bring him down or did he come down?"

"Today was different. Shots had been fired."

"You mean you brought him in as a witness?" There was a lilt of hope in Robertson's voice.

Keegan stared at him. The chief's main concern was to keep life calm for the political faction that had appointed him. Whenever Phil felt he was losing sight of the point of his job, acting vindictively, taking things too personally, he thought of Robertson and felt like an altar boy again. Robertson would not have wanted Liberati pressed about the stolen truck and his odd sales force even if the solution of the Enoch Hingle murder depended on it. He needed to be able to tell Liberati he was just a witness. Maybe he would issue a statement praising Liberati for cooperating with the police. Oh, what the hell.

"He was there when the shot was fired."

"Did he see the shooting?"

Together with Gruening and Albini, Liberati had made the full set of monkeys. A shot? He wasn't sure. He didn't even remember cussing DiNigro for carrying a gun. Under Tuttle's coaching, it was a wonder he even remembered his own name.

"What have you got on Enoch Hingle?" Robertson asked.

Keegan burned. He had no satisfactory answer for the chief, but what angered him was that he had none for himself. What they had was the body of a man who had been well known in Chicago twenty years ago. After a conviction for car theft, suspended, he had disappeared. He was said to have moved to the West Coast, but no trace of him had been picked up in Oregon. Keegan had asked Portland for anything they had on Hingle. The conclusion that Hingle had been a good boy since his youthful indiscretion seemed unavoidable. But then why all the phony ID? Why the gangland-style killing? The way he had died suggested that Hingle had been more lucky than legal. Gangland style. That brought Keegan's thoughts back to the trio in Liberati's office.

The three had refused Tuttle's offer to represent them, a decision that earned Keegan's grudging respect. They must not be as dumb as they looked, or they realized how serious their position really was, or both. Until they engaged counsel, there was no point in talking with them, even if they agreed to talk. That would have jeopardized the case against them. Keegan wished he knew if there *was* a case against them.

"It makes sense," Horvath said, when Keegan returned seething from Robertson's office. "The way Hingle died; those three. There could be a connection."

"You don't sound so sure."

"It's too easy. The three of them just sitting there waiting to be picked up."

"We didn't know they were there."

"They had to know we'd be coming there to talk to Liberati again. Any cop would recognize them fifty yards off."

"Why did you go there, Cy?"

Horvath's expression did not change. He had only one expression. "Iggie."

"How do you mean?"

"Iggie's paid to watch that lot. His son is assigned that route. Stevie. A truck is gone. Who knows?"

"You think Iggie's kid stole that truck?"

"I don't think anything. I was just checking."

"Stole the truck and dumped a dead body in it and parked it at Saint Hilary's?"

Cy turned away, but he was right and Keegan knew it. So why was he mad? He wasn't mad at Cy, he was sure of that, but how the hell was Horvath supposed to know? Keegan's stunned questions had put an end to the conversation, but Keegan knew he was going to have to find a way to let Cy know he had been right to check out anything and everything that might lead them to what had happened.

When Keegan learned that Roger Dowling was busy, he had telephoned Cy at home, hoping they could get together for a few beers and talk over what they knew. But it was Cy's bowling night.

So Keegan had had a jumbo hamburger with French fries and a large root beer and come home to his apartment where he made a cup of coffee. Long since cooled in the cup, it sat before him on the table. He dropped the end of his cigarette into the cup and its hissing extinction seemed a commentary on his inability to know where to go from here.

Iggie? Keegan pushed back from the table, liking and not liking the idea. It seemed an extension of Horvath's suspicion, but it was also a chance to talk to an old friend, and one who knew police business. He was also a guy, whether you liked it or not, who was mixed up in the murder under investigation.

Sally met him at the door and gave him a big hug and Keegan knew a moment's dizziness. Memories he had not known he had rushed in upon him and it was his dead wife he was holding in his arms.

"He's home, Phil. Dammit, I told you to call first. When he's home, you don't come. Remember? Like we agreed."

She stepped back, winked, and slapped his upper arms, both of them, using both her hands. Her head cocked and she smiled approvingly at him.

"You are growing old well, Phil Keegan."

"So are you, Sally."

She made a fist of her right hand and shook it under his face. "Never say that to a lady, Phil. You ought to know better."

"Okay. You're not growing old well."

Behind her was the chaos of the O'Brien household. Through the cluttered living room, newspapers scattered on the floor, through the dining room where the table still held the supper dishes, Iggie was visible in the den, stockinged feet up on a hassock, slumped into a Naugahyde chair, glaring at the television. Iggie had not looked to see who was at the door. There was always someone at the door in this house. Sally led the way and in the doorway of the den shouted to get Iggie's attention. He looked up, startled.

"I tell you, someone could walk into this place and rob us blind and you wouldn't even look up."

Iggie leaned forward and, looking around Sally, got a glimpse of Keegan. He struggled to his feet, and when Keegan got past Sally, he saw that Iggie was looking at him with real apprehension.

"What's wrong, Phil?"

"What's wrong?" Sally cried happily. "You left the department, that's what's wrong. Phil Keegan is here to beg you to come back. You're too late, Phil. A couple years ago I would have begged myself, but Ignatius has really done it, just as he said he would. He is a self-employed small businessman and business is good."

"Shut up, Sally."

"I love you, Ignatius." She punched him on the arm, hard.

"I mean let me and Keegan talk, all right?"

"I want to watch TV."

"So watch it. We'll talk in the kitchen."

The kitchen, like the dining room, bore witness to the meal recently completed. Where had all the little O'Briens gone?

"The older boys are catching a little nap before the night's work. The rest of them?" Iggie shrugged. "Who knows? Who wants to know anymore?"

Keegan was not deceived. Iggie and his wife ran a trim ship here. Well, not trim, but well disciplined.

"What do you make of those three characters Liberati had working for him, Iggie?"

"Phil, I knew something was fishy about those guys. Well, about one of them at least. DiNigro, the bastard who tried to take a shot at Horvath. But it never even crossed my mind that he'd be wanted. It should have. It hasn't been that long, Phil. Besides, it matters to me if that's the kind of people Liberati is employing."

"He employed you too, Iggie."

"That's right. What are you getting at?"

"Why did he?"

"You know why. You know what Owlize is. He was a client."

"With his connections, Liberati doesn't have to worry about thieves."

"Do you believe that stuff about Liberati, Phil? You know his family."

"I know his family."

But sooner or later a man had to be taken on his own terms, and Liberati had been a minor pain in the neck to the Fox River police ever since he took over the management of the family marina. Summer nights on the banks of the Fox River had always provided their share of demands for the police, and the marina, even under Carlo Liberati's management, had often been the scene of brawls brought on by too much beer in the sunshine. But the quality of the difficulties had altered since young Liberati took over. Drugs. No hard stuff, not that they knew about, but pills and pot in abundance had changed the flavor of the marina. It became an unsavory place.

This was the man who had opened a used-car lot in Fox River and had hired in one fell swoop three hoods as his sales force.

"You ever hear of Enoch Hingle, Iggie?"

"You mean lately? No. Funny how you forget about a kid like that and then he shows up and you remember it as if it were yesterday. What had he been doing all these years, Phil?"

"That's what I want to know."

"Well, you got ways of finding out."

To hell with it. Keegan dropped the subject. He would much rather drink beer and reminisce with Iggie about the old days. And that is what they did, joining Sally in the den, and they kept at it after she had gone off yawning to bed. They were both a little groggy when the CB unit began to blather. Iggie picked it up. It was the mode of communication between the Owlize patrols and home base.

"Dad, it's Stevie."

Keegan sat forward, alerted by the pitch of the young voice. It was Iggie's son Jack who was calling in.

"What's wrong, Jack?"

"Stevie, Dad. He's been shot."

Keegan was on the kitchen phone within seconds, putting in a call downtown. He and Iggie would go from here, but he wanted the Owlize VW under complete police control immediately.

14

To the eyes of Roger Dowling, St. Raphael's parish plant was a thing to behold. There were two school buildings flanking a side street closed to traffic during class hours and there was a church that seemed a block long, whose steeple lifted into the gray Chicago sky. Father Dowling got out of his car and stood on the walk. He let his eye be drawn up the steeple to the clouds beyond. More snow seemed to be on the way. He turned and started toward the rectory. The rectory more than anything else told him how different this parish was from his own.

It could have been mistaken for an apartment building, even an office building. It certainly did not look like a home. Roger Dowling came into a lobby-like hall where a receptionist looked at him over her counter and allowed her unreceptive air to alter. The Roman collar worked its magic in such a place.

"I am Roger Dowling."

"Yes, Father." The girl seemed a high school student, but could not have been. Twenty at most. This wasn't much of a job for her and he did not blame her for not pretending otherwise.

"Is Father Doremus in? He's expecting me."

"I'll ring his suite."

On one wall of the lobby was a huge picture of the cardinal, with a light trained on it. It was a touched-up photograph, as far as Roger Dowling could make out. There was no picture of the cardinal in the St. Hilary rectory, a sin of omission at most, though Roger Dowling had not decided not to hang one. It simply had not entered his mind. He did have a picture of the pope in his study, a candid photo, in color, a memento of his Chicago visit.

"He'll come down," the girl announced.

Some minutes later the doors of an elevator opened and a priest who looked vaguely familiar emerged and came toward Roger Dowling with outstretched hand, the gleam of recognition in his eye.

"Father Dowling! Welcome to Saint Raphael's. Here, let me take that."

Rather than fight him for it, Father Dowling let Doremus take his overnight bag. They got into the elevator and Doremus punched 3. "There is one guest room on the street floor, but I don't recommend it. Too noisy."

"I haven't been able to reach Mrs. Ludwig."

Doremus had to think who that might be.

"The sister of the deceased, Father. Enoch Hingle's sister."

"Yes, of course. Mrs. Ludwig. I've been so busy getting ready to go to . . ." Doremus stopped and his eyes widened with forgetfulness.

"Saint Hilary's. Fox River. Mrs. Murkin is expecting you."

"The funeral is at Mooney's. I mean the body."

A rosary was scheduled for that evening at seven-thirty and it seemed that it was at the funeral home that Father Dowling was first to meet the surviving sister of Enoch Hingle. Repeated tries failed to get an answer from the Ludwig telephone. Perhaps it was just as well. Roger Dowling preferred to speak with the woman in person, and he had hoped this would be at her home. But there was perhaps something to be said for discussing her brother in the somber atmosphere of a funeral parlor. Had she spent the day in seclusion, mourning her dead brother?

"I was working."

Mrs. Ludwig answered his question without any apparent sense that her answer might surprise him. She arrived at Mooney's about ten minutes after seven and the young Mooney, Mark, ushered her into the room where Father Dowling had been reading his breviary since shortly before the hour. Young Mooney had been relieved that he did not have to entertain the priest and he seemed almost as relieved that he could deliver Mrs. Ludwig over to Father Dowling.

"Where do you work?"

She worked in a travel bureau whose offices were in a bank building on North Michigan. Her head tipped to one side, as if to catch between ear and shoulder the telephone that was the instrument of her trade. Florida. Mexico. The Caribbean. Hawaii.

"Sometimes I think the whole city is heading out of here in search of the sun. Everyone but me, that is." Her mouth's set was downward at the edges and a wrinkled omega formed between her brows, both indices of self-pity perhaps.

The left eye drifted slightly whenever she tried to fix her gaze on Father Dowling.

"I thought travel agents traveled a lot."

"Some do. Those that work for large firms. I don't. I was in Sarasota once. In June. All expenses paid. Big deal. All I enjoyed was the air-conditioning in the motel."

"Enoch's death must have been a great shock to you." Even as he said the words, Roger Dowling feared he had not kept irony from his voice. But Mrs. Ludwig's forehead wrinkled and she nodded.

"Do you know how I heard? WMAQ. I like country western and I hate news. They don't have much news, just on the hour. That's when I heard it. You can imagine the shock. Not that many people remember Enoch anymore."

"Will your husband be coming tonight?"

She looked at him suspiciously, but the left eye turned away and then she did too. "We're separated."

Roger Dowling had the grim certainty that this meant Ludwig had left her. "Any children?"

"No. Thank God," she added, her tone defiant. "So I support myself. That's why I'm not a contributor at Saint Raphael's."

"That's all right," Roger Dowling said, and he could imagine Monsignor Lothian twitch in pain beside some blue-green pool in Florida.

"I've attended your Mass."

He did not correct her, then wondered if he should have. Clearly she was not a regular attendant at her parish church if she thought he was one of the curates. Did she perhaps mistake him for Monsignor Lothian himself? He suggested that St. Raphael's was not the same as the parish in which she and Enoch had grown up.

"Not at all. Have you been in that neighborhood lately?"

"What do you mean?"

"Black." She whispered it, actually bringing a cupped hand to the side of her mouth. "All black."

"When did you last see Enoch?"

"They showed him to me yesterday."

"I meant alive."

She thought about it, closing her eyes and tipping her head back. Was she counting the years?

"October."

"Last October?"

"It was before Thanksgiving, I know that. I suggested we have Thanksgiving dinner together. He could chip in and I would cook and we would eat in my apartment. We've been doing that ever since Ludwig . . . for quite a number of years. Of course Enoch never liked to promise anything in advance. He didn't like to be tied down."

"Did he visit Chicago often?"

Her frown formed chevrons in her nose. "How do you mean, visit?"

"I heard he had been living in Oregon."

"Who in the world told you that? He went out there when he was a kid, right after high school. He wanted to get away from everything. But he was back within a year. Who told you he lived in Oregon?"

"He lived in Chicago?"

She opened her purse and took out a package of cigarettes. "Is it okay to smoke in here?"

Roger Dowling told her to smoke if she wanted to. He would have liked to light his pipe, but it was too close to the time for the rosary.

"He changed his name. After a little trouble he had, just before he went to Oregon, he wanted a new start. At the time I wasn't very sympathetic. Later on I understood how he felt. Ludwig. Why do I keep his name? But going back to my maiden name didn't make much sense. Enoch told me I could use any name I felt like."

"You mean have it changed legally?"

"Why? He said he never did. All you have to do is establish credit in a new name and it's yours. I never did that though."

"What name did he use?"

He wondered if the name she mentioned was one of those represented on the credit cards and other ID that had been found on Enoch Hingle's body. I am legion. Surely the police would be checking out all those names to see if they led anywhere.

Dowling said, "It will make a difference in discovering what he may have left."

"Money?" Her laugh was short and sad. "Not Enoch. Whenever we did see each other the visit ended with him trying to put the bite on me. And I always gave him something. Little brother, big sister. It's funny. No matter how old we got, that's what we were. And how can you refuse your little brother?"

It was one of the most redeeming things she had said, and Roger Dowling decided the remark canceled the apparent callousness of her working on the day of her brother's wake. She seemed to read his thoughts. Her eyes were damp when she turned to him after snuffing out her cigarette.

"In order to get tomorrow off, I had to work today. Can you imagine? Nobody does anybody any favors, not anymore. The world has changed since Enoch and I were young, I can tell you that."

When they went into the room where the body was on

view there were three people waiting for them, two of whom were Mooneys. F. X., the elder, drew Father Dowling aside.

"Not much of a crowd," he said out of the corner of his mouth.

Lorraine Ludwig had suddenly realized the same thing. She went to the prie-dieu in front of the casket and threw herself on her knees and began to weep loudly. The younger Mooney went to stand beside her, as comforter, perhaps as subduer if she became hysterical. The other mourner was a middle-aged man, heavy-set, who seemed determined not to notice Mrs. Ludwig's grief, or perhaps to regard it as the expected thing. F. X. Mooney and Roger Dowling took up positions by the disconsolate sister and the priest began the recitation of the rosary.

There is something soothing in the repetition of a formula of prayer. The familiar round of the beads, the commemoration of the sorrowful mysteries, seemed to reconcile Lorraine to the loss of her brother. The casket was shut after all, thank God. Roger Dowling looked forward to a minuscule crowd at the funeral Mass and a lonely trip to the cemetery. Would there be anyone beside himself, Mrs. Ludwig, and the undertakers? It was clear that Enoch Hingle's sister had not taken on the task of assembling pallbearers. She told Father Dowling this after they had finished saying the rosary.

"I thought he had so many friends. . . ." Her voice broke and in her eyes swam the realization that she herself was not surrounded by a coterie of friends. Where, after all, were her friends this night? She turned away from Father Dowling and the other mourner came forward to take her hand. Roger Dowling was distracted by the unctuous voice of the undertaker.

"I'm sorry if I sounded less than forthcoming on the telephone, Father Dowling. I didn't understand your interest in the deceased." F. X. Mooney had a lunar-landscape face, pocked, thin, of indeterminate color. His luxuriant brows made his sockets seem more cadaverous, and the eyes that looked up at Father Dowling were intent and unblinking.

"How many times had he been shot, Mr. Mooney?"

"I didn't ask. It was quite a job, pasting the body together. There was never any question of there being a viewing. Of course she had to see the body, for purposes of identification. She took that a good deal better than she did this."

"Apparently they weren't close."

Mooney's expression changed. Mrs. Ludwig joined them. Father Dowling turned to see the pudgy mourner leaving the room.

"A friend of Enoch's?" he asked Mrs. Ludwig.

"I guess. He had trouble speaking. But he said one thing that made sense."

"What was that?" F. X. Mooney asked, and his voice wavered between cheeriness and the sepulchral, let the hearer make her choice.

"The snow. It's terrible out there. That's why people didn't come. Everyone thinks everyone else will be here, so it doesn't matter if they stay home."

"What do you mean, he had trouble speaking?" Roger Dowling asked.

"He stuttered."

15

FEENEY sat in a straight-back chair in the basement of St. Hilary rectory. The chair was cushioned with an old pillow, and Feeney had placed it behind the furnace where, when he tipped back, he could lean against the wall and put his feet up on the oil burner. That way there was no chance of falling and he could drift into sleep if he wanted to without worry. Without worry about anything but Marie Murkin, that is.

Feeney had been hired in the fall by Father Dowling as more or less of a janitor and maintenance man for the rectory and school. The church was looked after by Mrs. Murkin herself. She didn't want someone like Timothy Feeney wandering around the church. That was the message of her manner; she hadn't said it outright. But Timothy Feeney, after sixty-six years at the bottom of the pile, had developed antennae that enabled him to pick up insults only dogs were meant to hear.

"Sixty-six?" Mrs. Murkin had said. "Why don't you apply for Social Security?"

"I don't have any."

"Nonsense. Everybody has Social Security. You can't hold a job without it."

"You can in Joliet," Feeney said.

That shut her up, if only because the priest was there, Dowling, her boss. And his boss too. From time to time Feeney reminded Mrs. Murkin of that fact. His boss was the pastor, not the housekeeper. They were both employees here and he wasn't taking any orders from her. So she chose to ignore him. Feeney felt invisible, shoveling the walks, sweeping the aisles of the school where people his own age and older fooled around all day as if they were kids again. The school reminded him of the prison in which he had spent so many years and that was both its attraction and repulsion. He much preferred the parish house, sitting in this chair behind the furnace, daydreaming, letting time go by. He had long ago acquired the art of just letting time go by, permitting it to take the least toll on him as it passed. He had thought of setting up sleeping quarters down here in the rectory basement, but Marie Murkin had raised so much hell at the suggestion that Dowling asked Feeney to stay in the caretaker's apartment in the school. A matter of insurance, he said. He didn't want the school to be unattended throughout the night.

So Feeney stayed in the school. What choice did he have? And what luck would he have had trying to explain that a man his age was afraid to be alone in that building all night? The reason he slept so much during the day was that he slept so little at night. He didn't even undress. He locked the door of the caretaker's room, which was on the first floor of the school, and he did not turn on any lights. There were night lights in the school, for whatever deterrent effect they might have, but Feeney did not intend to attract any nocturnal visitors to his own quarters.

Oh, the sounds he heard behind the locked door of his room, his ear pressed to the door. Odd noises in the corridor, windy sighing sounds, creaks and banging of pipes as the temperature lowered. The music of the radiators on a winter night was eerie and he could imagine that the ghosts of all the kids who had put in time in this place had come back to haunt it. Fanciful? He had had plenty of time to develop his imagination, living in a cage, but he did not regard imagination as his friend. He could not really believe it was only imagination. Querulous old voices, the cries of kids at play, the complaints of the walls and floors, the sound of the wind whining around the corners of the building—none of this kept him company or diminished his sense of loneliness.

Out there was the hostile world from which he had been protected by walls and steel doors and bars at Joliet. They had all complained about being there, no one was guilty of anything, and the point of survival was to get on the other side of the wall and be free. Feeney told himself that he had never shared that attitude, but he had, on the inside. Once he actually was on the outside he realised how unfit for it he had become. The chaplain, Rabb, had made the contact with Father Dowling and Feeney had come to Fox River on a straight line. He had no desire to experiment with his freedom and not because he was afraid they would slap him back inside if he wasn't a good boy. He wanted to get somewhere where he would belong, and that was what St. Hilary's was for him, and to hell with Marie Murkin. If there had been guards keeping him in the school at night, and keeping other people out, he could have slept like a baby. But the only thing between him and a world he no longer understood was the door he himself shut and locked. So he remained dressed and sat up all night and listened to the school speak.

That is why he had seen the two trucks pull up in the street outside that night. At first he had thought the second was pushing the first, but when they undid the chain he saw that the first had been pulling the second. He stood some feet back from his window as he watched them. A street lamp provided lighting enough for his room throughout the night and he wasn't sure whether it made him visible from outside. Not that anyone looked his way.

There had been two of them and both had been riding in the front truck. No, three. The third had slipped under the back bumper of the lead vehicle and he was being very careful. The other two stood there waiting and Feeney could sense their watchfulness. But there was the unmistakable sound of metal being dragged over metal and then the third man slid out from underneath and handed the chain to one of the others. He pitched it into the back of the lead truck, making a hell of a noise, and Feeney thought that the one who had undone the chain was going to deck him. He actually started to swing but the third one grabbed his arm and they all froze for a minute and then relaxed. They all got into the lead truck and closed the doors so softly Feeney couldn't hear them. Besides, he was distracted by the glinting arc of something thrown from the cab of the truck. It sailed through the air and hit the snow soundlessly and then the truck pulled away. Its motor had been on all along and the clouds of exhaust seemed to hang in the frozen air. Feeney stood there for half an hour staring at the truck they had apparently abandoned on the street.

It was empty. He did not wonder why the truck had been left there. Again, training. He had learned to keep curiosity at a minimum, to ask no questions, to keep his mouth shut.

That had been in Joliet, of course, but he had felt instinctively that those silent men in the street were more like him than they were like the rest of people wandering around in the world. They could not have been up to any good in the dead of night and acting with such furtiveness. He kept vigil throughout the night; the abandoned truck gave him a sort of excuse for not going to bed. He did fall asleep for a couple of hours, but when he looked outside dark was lifting in the false dawn and the truck was still there. It was just a truck now. If he had not seen the odd way in which it arrived, it would not have held his interest for a minute.

The next morning, when he shoveled the walks, he kept right on moving past the truck, but he gave it a pretty good going over out of the corner of his eye. He had seen the blood that had oozed under the door before freezing. How did he know it was blood? He just knew. So he kept on moving, more resolved than ever to curb his curiosity about that truck and to tell no one what he had seen the night before. He also calculated the trajectory of the object that had been thrown from the other truck as it drove away. There was no mark on the snow where it had landed. He would check that out later, if at all.

Throughout the morning he waited for someone to notice the truck—Father Dowling, Mrs. Murkin, someone—but you would have thought it was a permanent feature of the neighborhood. In midmorning he went over to the church and jimmied open the money box on the pamphlet rack, hoping Mrs. Murkin would notice and start yipping and yapping and then the truck would become visible for her. But she just babbled to Dowling and that was that. The priest went over to the church with her. When they came back, Feeney, listening in his chair behind the furnace, waited for the big discovery of the truck. Nothing.

It made him mad. It seemed a deliberate snub to him,

the fact that Mrs. Murkin refused to notice the truck. It was the first time she had failed to stick her nose into something, probably because this more or less concerned her. When she came downstairs to the freezer and took out some meat, Feeney had half a mind to lean out and say boo and scare her out of her skivvies. But he preferred the amusement of being down there without her knowing it. Besides, the meat gave him an idea. He would do something she could not ignore.

After lunch, he heard her private stairway creak as she went up to her room for her afternoon snooze. Feeney gathered up an armful of jams and jellies and carried them upstairs. He took them outside and dug a hole in the snow and buried them. He did the same thing with the pork chops she had been defrosting. Then, to make sure that even Marie Murkin would put two and two together, he trudged through the snow to the abandoned truck, careful to avoid the spot where the thrown object had landed. Back in the house, he made tracks, with overshoes on and with overshoes off. Satisfied, he went back to his room in the school and waited for things to happen.

And they did. Feeney kept out of the way, particularly after they pulled the body out of the truck. No wonder Mrs. Murkin had fainted in the street when she peeked into the cab. He smiled at the memory of it. It served her right. After ignoring the truck all day, she had gotten too nosy for her own good. In subsequent days, Feeney read the newspaper reports on the body and wondered if they really knew as little as those stories contained. He tried to hear whether Mrs. Hospers or any of the old birds knew anything. Not that he could put the question to them. Even less so to Mrs. Murkin. But he resented the fact that it had not even occurred to her to mention his name to the police. He would have denied seeing anything, just as she and Dowling had, but they should at least have asked him. It made him sore.

That is why, when he checked his calculations and crossed the yard slowly, feeling beneath the snow with his feet and finding the gun, he slipped it into his pocket and had no intention of telling anyone he had found it or where it had come from. To hell with them. If he was the invisible man, then that is what he was. And the invisible man would not speak either. He would show them.

Besides, it was safer that way, keeping his mouth shut.

16

THE BODY of Stevie O'Brien was found in an abandoned ice shack on the half-melted surface of Lake Peavy by a drunken vagrant who had unwittingly risked drowning in order to claim the shack for a much-needed sleep. Horvath questioned the man in a booth of the Peavy Café. His name was Howard.

"Howard what?"

The stubble of his beard was salt and pepper, his eyes were red-rimmed, his mouth sagged in toothless weakness. His gaze drifted by Horvath.

"Howard Charles."

"Which is your first name?" Horvath had thought he heard a catch between the two names that might have been a comma. His first name was Howard. He held his coffee mug with both hands and drank from it as if he were taking medicine. He put it down with a clunk.

"God, that's hot."

"Tell me the whole story."

Howard Charles picked up the mug but did not drink. Putting it back on the table, he cupped it in his hands. He sat up straight for a moment, then slumped back into the posture of resignation. Had he been tempted by the importance Horvath's question conferred upon him? It was one temptation he resisted. He had not resisted the temptation to rob the body of Stevie O'Brien.

The Peavy Café might be a booming place in summer, but now in winter it did a meager business. It was a wonder it stayed open at all. The dining room in which Horvath sat with Howard Charles was empty. The room was all windows, windows with small panes, so that Horvath's view of the frozen lake was a composite of small squares, a simplistic jigsaw puzzle. He could see the ice shack, tipped now, sunk into water that lapped one corner. The planks and ladders that had been laid on the ice to gain access to the shack and to Stevie's body were still there. Horvath wondered if they would try to retrieve them or let them become part of the springtime flotsam and jetsam that washed up on the shores of Lake Peavy. How easily Stevie's body might have slid beneath the surface during this late February thaw and not been found until spring.

"What time was it when you found the body?"

"Last night."

"What time last night?" Even as he asked the question, Horvath recognized in Howard Charles a man for whom the clock was no longer a point of reference, a constraint, a goad, a measure. Night and day were sufficiently fine-grained indicators for him. "Where were you before you went out to the ice shack?"

"I thought it was a portable john. The kind construction companies use."

Any pot in a storm? Horvath wondered if Howard Charles had planned to spend the night in an outdoor toilet. Well, the ice shack wouldn't have been any more comfortable. What Howard had found when he pushed open the door of the shack was a body.

"I didn't know he was dead. Not at first. Then I thought he must have frozen to death."

"So you robbed him?"

"I checked for identification," Howard corrected.

When he found the wallet with two hundred dollars in it, Howard took it and started back the way he had come. A sheriff's patrol came upon him weaving down the middle of a county road. Howard tried to run when they put the spotlight on him, so of course they had picked him up. It was the two hundred dollars that made him more than a common tramp. That and Stevie's wallet, which he had also taken.

"How do I know the man wasn't alive when you got to that ice shack, Howard? Maybe you killed him for that two hundred dollars."

Howard simply shook his head; no indignation, no pretense that this would have been unheard of. "No. He was already dead."

Horvath knew that. Even Phelps was fairly forthcoming in saying the body had been dead for at least twenty-four hours. Of course the assistant coroner had immediately backed away from such facile conviction, but his first horseback guess was very likely right. Besides, Stevie had been shot, and Howard Charles would have traded a gun for booze before he would have used it to kill someone. Horvath had the awful thought that the .22 that had killed Stevie was now at the bottom of Lake Peavy and would never provide a clue or lead in the case. Pretty damned convenient, shoot a man and then drop the weapon down the ice hole into the frozen deeps. Was it the same gun that had been used to kill Enoch Hingle? It was difficult not to see the two killings as related, although what the relation was would have been difficult to say. Horvath hoped the killer had kept the weapon. He might then use it on a third person before they got hold of him, of course, but if the weapon was at the bottom of Lake Peavy they were going to need an awful lot of luck.

Howard Charles craned his neck to see what was going on in the next room where Iggie O'Brien was alternately raging and weeping over what had happened to his son. Horvath would have preferred staying with Keegan while he talked with his old friend Iggie about his murdered son, but someone had to do the routine questioning of Howard Charles. Iggie was far more likely to know something that would provide a clue. At the moment he was bellowing with anger, vowing to track down the bastard who had killed Stevie and string him up from a tree. Keegan had offered to tell Sally. Sally had to be told. Iggie seemed to think that as long as he didn't tell his wife their son was dead Stevie was somehow still alive. But he had seen Stevie's body and his shoulders had shaken with sobs as he stood over the dead frozen body of his second son.

Horvath decided to let the vagrant go. Howard Charles seemed certain he was still under arrest. There would have been no point to it. Hold him as a witness? To what? They knew Stevie was dead and he had been for hours prior to Howard Charles's stumbling across him. Howard's major regret was that they had confiscated the money he had stolen from Stevie. Horvath took a five from his wallet and gave it to the vagrant.

"Don't spend it all in one place."

The money disappeared as if by a magician's trick. Howard nodded in thanks and was on his feet. His eyes glistened. Horvath had no doubt the man would invest the five in cheap wine.

"Why don't you have something to eat before you go, Howard. Some toast and coffee. A sandwich."

Howard's hesitation was brief. No. He had to get going. And he went. Horvath, still seated in the booth, watched Howard accelerate as he shuffled toward the door, the outside, a liquor store. Where was his drunken traveling taking him if not to some bitter end like that Stevie O'Brien had found? But nobody escapes death forever. Horvath shook away these uncharacteristic thoughts and went into the other room. Keegan had just announced to Iggie that he was going to telephone Sally. Iggie said nothing, turning toward Horvath, and Keegan went away.

"That goddamn Liberati," Iggie said to Horvath.

"How do you mean?" Cy sat on the stool next to O'Brien's and shook his head when the grandmotherly lady behind the counter lifted her coffee pot in a question.

"Think about it, Horvath. You're the detective, not me, not anymore. This is two of them."

"What did Enoch Hingle have to do with Liberati?"

"You tell me. He was found in a truck stolen off Liberati's lot."

"That's right. It was stolen from Liberati."

"Says who?"

"You think Liberati killed Hingle, put him in one of his trucks, and parked it by Saint Hilary's?"

But the truck had been towed to that location. Suddenly Horvath had one of those ideas he kicked himself for not having earlier. The truck could have been towed by another vehicle from Liberati's lot.

"You tell me," Iggie said again.

"How many vehicles did Liberati report missing?"

"None! Think about that, Horvath. A truck is stolen and he doesn't even notice? I don't believe it."

"Only the one vehicle is missing?"

"Who knows?"

"Do you?"

"Ask Liberati."

But what Horvath did that afternoon was to go to Liberati's lot with two men from the police garage. Liberati came out onto the porch of the mobile home when they drove in. His face was a mask of sorrow.

"It's true what I hear about Stevie O'Brien?"

"Where did you hear it?"

But it was his secretary Charmaine who answered. Tuttle. Liberati looked suspiciously at the two men who had come with Horvath, but the lieutenant led Liberati and Charmaine back into the office. He wanted the inspection of the vehicles in the lot to go on unimpeded. The office seemed empty without Albini, Gruening, and DiNigro. Horvath said this.

"Those bums," Liberati growled.

"I liked them," Charmaine said. She looked at Horvath with sudden grief. "And I loved Stevie. Is Tuttle telling the truth?"

Horvath told Liberati and the girl that Stevie O'Brien had been found dead in an ice shack on Lake Peavy, shot with a .22.

"A .22!" Charmaine cried.

"Who found him?" Liberati asked, looking at Horvath, but Cy was certain Liberati could sense the stunned look on his secretary's face.

"What about a .22?" Horvath asked the secretary.

Liberati didn't look at her, he didn't say a thing, but Horvath could have sworn he heard the man tell the girl to shut up.

"Tell me," Horvath urged Charmaine.

Liberati adopted a pained smile and shook his head

with disgust. "There are at least a million .22s in the country, Charmaine. It is the most numerous weapon in the United States of America."

That is when it clicked for Horvath. The newspaper stories, the prizes; it was something he had always known. Liberati was an ace of the target range. Among hand guns, he was nationally ranked with the .22. It was one of those times when Horvath's impassive countenance helped. There was no sign of recognition on his face and no metaphorical bulb clicked above his head.

"How many .22s do you own, Liberati?"

"Lots of them."

"Where do you keep them?"

"At home." Charmaine stirred and he added, "I keep a few here."

He kept half a dozen in his office, two of them mounted on plaques, guns he had used to win the prize inscribed in the bronze plate of the plaque.

"They all here?"

"What do you mean?"

"Are you missing any weapons? Better count them. You didn't know you were missing a truck until we told you."

"They're all here."

"Is that right, Charmaine?"

But the secretary was once more her boss's right-hand girl. "How do I know? It looks like all of them."

"It is all of them," Liberati said.

"Enoch Hingle was killed with a .22. Now Stevie O'Brien. That's two."

"What's the connection?"

"The .22."

And then Jaspers and Anselm came in. They had found what Horvath had hoped they would. It was a guess for now, but it wouldn't be for long, Horvath was sure of that. In any case, he had instructed Anselm carefully on their drive to Liberati's. And Anselm spoke with authority.

"There's no doubt about it, Lieutenant. It was used to pull the truck in which the body was found. We'll run tests on paint samples, but I'd stake my reputation on it."

"That's another connection, Liberati. You."

"What the hell are you talking about?"

"Charmaine," Horvath said, throwing Liberati's coat at the car dealer. "Phone Tuttle and tell him his client is under arrest. Suspicion of homicide."

Liberati caught his coat and decided not to protest. Perhaps the mention of Tuttle decided him. He could pay lawyers to argue his case, why should he do it himself? On the ride downtown, Horvath sat in back with Liberati. They would get a warrant and check out Liberati's collection of .22 pistols. They would dust down the truck Anselm felt had towed the one in which Enoch Hingle's body had been found.

"It's a bad break for you, Liberati."

Liberati, arms folded, stared straight ahead.

"If your salesmen weren't in custody, you could pin the shootings on them. But they couldn't have killed Stevie O'Brien."

Liberati's lids fluttered, like a sleeping person's having a dream. He had decided not to say something.

"That's right," Horvath said. "Let Tuttle do your talking."

The chuckle that emanated from Liberati, perhaps meant to be theatrical, sounded genuine.

17

EVELYN made Jennie a breakfast of cornflakes and toast and instant coffee and went back to preparing herself for her own day while her mother ate. Jennie's appetite increased with age, and an earlier incident, another one of those damnable interviews with the Hospers woman, had taught Evelyn never to drop her mother off at St. Hilary's school with anything less than an enormous breakfast behind her. Jennie was perfectly capable of making the whining insinuation that her daughter was systematically starving her to death. Evelyn herself would have a bite at her desk, coffee and a Danish, more than enough breakfast for her. She ran her palms along the bulge of her thighs and resolved to lay off the bourbon and 7-up; she was putting on weight again.

The realization filled her with an obscure rage, directed at the universe, herself, the fact that she was growing older and that her body developed odd lumps and bulges now more or less independently of any caloric indulgence on her part. And her make-up took so long now. When she was young, she had disdained all cosmetics other than lipstick. Now cosmetics—eyeshadow, rouge, elaborate shiny substances for the lips—were an in thing and Evelyn was glad. Once any make-up drew attention and the assumption had been that a woman had something to hide if she covered her face lavishly. Young or not, it was her eyelashes that had always given Evelyn trouble, second only to that given her by her eyebrows. Her left eyebrow did not match her right; the latter was thin, the former thick. She did what she could with a pencil and plucker but she was never really satisfied with the result. As for her eyelashes, well, if she could not have worn artificial ones she would have been in deep trouble. Unadorned, her eyes peered from her sockets with a startled expression, and if she attempted to compensate for this by lowering her mascaraed lids, the result was a sleepy, almost drugged, expression. Hence the lashes. But if there was anything that felt falser than a false eyelash, Evelyn did not want to know what it was.

When she was finally done, she went into the kitchen to prod Jennie. Her mother had hardly touched her cereal and her coffee looked untasted. She was nibbling on a piece of toast while she read the morning paper.

"I wonder if he's a relative," she mused aloud in response to Evelyn's cry of anger.

"Will you for the love of Pete finish your breakfast? We have to go. I'll be late. Again!"

"Liberati," Jennie said, looking up at her daughter.

Evelyn's mouth had opened to say something but now remained that way in surprise.

"What do you mean, Liberati?"

"They've arrested him."

Evelyn snatched the paper unceremoniously from her mother's hand. Robert Liberati arrested as suspect in two recent shootings. There was a picture of him, obviously taken on some earlier occasion. He was wearing a windbreaker, his hair tossed by the wind, and he smiled into the camera, looking down at the lens with an expression that brought back memories of summer fun years and years ago. When Evelyn saw that one of the shootings was of Enoch Hingle, she sat down at the table and sipped her mother's coffee.

"At first I thought it was Carlo," Jennie said. "I don't suppose he'll come today."

Evelyn only half heard what her mother said, her attention on the newspaper story. Robbie Liberati, imagine! But she could imagine him killing someone. He had had an absolutely flammable temper and the big smile and affected control made his anger all the more surprising and overwhelming when it burst forth. Evelyn would never forget the episode that had spelled the end of her relations with Robbie Liberati.

It had been, how long ago? It didn't matter, there was no need to depress herself with exactitude as to how many years had passed since the summer she had gone with Robbie. Suffice it to say it had been after her divorce, her first divorce, and in the manner of the new divorcée she had been trying desperately to get back to where she had been before she married. She learned later how futile an effort this was, but that summer she hadn't known, so of course she had spent a lot of time at the Liberati marina. The beach there had been the scene of so many happy hours of her girlhood. It had seemed fated that Robbie Liberati should be much in evidence, strutting about on the burning sands in the briefest of swimming trunks, his naturally dark skin rendered a rich bronze by the sun. He was hairy and Evelyn would have thought she didn't like hairy men, but somehow he was different. Her campaign to catch his eye took three days, but she was successful. When she told him she was divorced, she saw his ambiguous reaction. On the one hand, he disapproved. On the other, she clearly took on for him an attraction she would not otherwise have had, and she knew what it was. He could never become really serious about her. There could never be any question of marriage. The divorce.

But if she seemed available, no threat of permanency, that did not mean he was incapable of jealousy. On the one hand, he never properly introduced her to his parents—that was part of the Catholic thing, she supposed: what would they make of their son going out with a divorcée? On the other hand, he expected her to be true to him as though she were his wife. And to be available. Whenever he felt like it, she was supposed to be ready. Well, she had liked that, at first. Part of the therapy she needed was to feel wanted, desired, possessed. But his attitude became oppressive after a time, then boring. There was excitement to be had from deceiving him, if you could call it that. She went out with other men and even as she did she knew he would never stand for it. With anyone else, she might have used his jealousy as a lever into marriage, but she knew, without quite knowing how she knew it, that he would never in a million years marry a divorcée. Even if he did, he would not consider it a real marriage. She had as much of him as she was ever likely to get. So there were other men. And he found out.

He struck her. Hard. With his open hand, but it literally knocked her down. She was so stunned she had not even screamed. She looked up at him from the floor—they were in her apartment—shocked, horrified, and frightened. In that moment, as he stared down at her with rage, his eyes smoldering like the villain's in a melodrama, she believed that he meant to kill her, that some Sicilian code she could never hope to understand now gave him the right to kill her with impunity. She heard herself telling him she was sorry. It was this, far more than the memory of the blow, that humiliated her afterward. To let him strike her and then to crawl begging for forgiveness! Of course he considered her beyond forgiveness. That had been the end of it. The blow that had sent her reeling across her living room had been his way of writing an end to their affair.

She had hated him ever since, in absentia, over the years, but at the same time the memory of that odd relationship, in which she had always been at a disadvantage, proved unfading. The first time she realized she had the image of Robbie Liberati in her mind's eye whenever she listened to Sinatra records, she had tried to feel anger and disgust, but she could not. He was the only man who had ever struck her. Maybe she was a little kinky, remaining fascinated by him, but her fascination had been controllable. She had never felt an impulse to look him up again. She had soon remarried and the next time she divorced, she knew there was no point in looking backward. The past was there to be cherished, in memory, but it could no longer be rejoined. So Robbie Liberati had taken on a special role in her tenseless self-indulgent reveries.

"It's not Carlo," Jennie said when Evelyn put the paper aside.

"Who the hell is Carlo?"

"Carlo Liberati. I see him at Saint Hilary's." Her mother's look became sly. "The old goat has a crush on me."

"So I've heard," Evelyn said, the painful memory of sessions with Edna Hospers assailing her momentarily. "Is his name Carlo?"

"Carlo Liberati. He owns a place down by the river, for boats. You used to go swimming there when you were a kid."

"What's he like?"

Jennie giggled. "A man."

Evelyn tried not to lose her patience. Did it never end, this silly game between male and female? There had been a time, when she was very young, when Evelyn had imagined that a woman of the age she herself had now reached would have put all such matters out of her head. How wrong she had been. And the same was true of men. Why did it seem so comic? Because it was pointless, mating to no purpose? But Evelyn had always mated to no purpose other than the deed itself. She had never wanted kids, even the one she had had, the one who had died.

"Is he a widower?"

"That's right," Jennie chirped, pushing back from the table. "Let's go. I want to see if he comes in today."

"Does he live with his son?"

"It's the other way around. At least that's what he says."

"Where is his home?"

"I've never been there."

"And he's never been here. But then, I suppose he has a crush on all the ladies."

This stung Jennie into angry denial. She was still at it in the car, insisting that Carlo treated her alone with affection and interest. Finally she subsided and rode in injured silence. When they arrived at the school Evelyn said, "You should invite him over. He must be very lonely and now, with this trouble with his son . . ."

"I'm not baby-sitting Carlo Liberati," Jennie said, slowly getting out of the car.

"It was just a thought." Evelyn tried to make her tone convey skepticism, as when she had cast doubt on Carlo Liberati's exclusive interest in Jennie.

Jennie slammed the car door hard and walked in her birdlike yet still oddly agile way up the shoveled walk to the school door.

18

THE MURDER of Enoch Hingle and the theme it suggested of the vanity of human hopes and aspirations, particularly of youthful dreams, ignited in Marcus Riehle the long-discarded notion that he was destined to be a noveliest. That the theme of the thwarting of young dreams should have served as the reviver of his own dead dream possessed an irony that, he felt, could only bode well for his effort. Not that he intended to rely only on his own experience. The autobiographical novel, he had learned from previous attempts to write one, is a trap for the fledgling. Oh, doubtless he would rely in part on his own experience, how could he do otherwise, but in the main he meant to stand outside the events of his story and see them with the calm and comprehending eye of omniscience. And this meant he needed objective facts. He would blend the factual research of a Zola or

Sinclair Lewis with the soul of Scott Fitzgerald. His hero would be an irresistible blend of Enoch Hingle and Marcus Riehle.

The decision to attend the wake seemed inevitable once he saw matters in this way. But, when he arrived at Mooney's and found the viewing room all but empty, he knew a moment of panic. He had imagined himself blending into the throng, listening, watching, taking the mental notes that would enable him to transform the event into a memorable fictional scene. Flight seemed the only answer; he did not want to be conspicuous. Besides, there was the matter of taste. It was ghoulish to be attending wakes and funerals in quest of fictional grist. But he vacillated between the ideas of going and staying. He kept his belted raincoat on as an outward sign of this inward indecision. The younger Mooney hovered too, perhaps made uneasy by Riehle's hesitancy. And then the pathos of the situation dawned on Marcus Riehle. My God! The youthful athletic hero, the toast of the Chicago sports pages, having been gunned down in Fox River, is laid out in an empty room, ignored, unsung, unwept for. It was the obverse of the scene in Bellow's *Seize the Day.* Marcus Riehle felt the gentle breath of impending fame and acclaim on his neck. Dear Lord, this was it. This was what was meant by the cliché of inspiration. He had found his perfect subject at last.

Still wearing his raincoat, he went into the viewing room and sat in the back. A woman he assumed must be a relative of Hingle's came, flanked by a priest and a Mooney, threw herself on the kneeler before the casket, and burst into tears. Marcus Riehle's throat constricted in empathy with the woman. How unbearably sad, this large dimly lit room with its rows and rows of chairs and this mere handful of people. Riehle had a momentary image of his own obsequies and again there was the fusion of the personal and objective that would be the hallmark of his novel.

He had been so absorbed in the pathetic figure of the woman sobbing before the closed casket that he did not at first recognize the priest. Father Dowling? What was he doing here? Did the fact that the body of Enoch Hingle had been found outside his rectory give him jurisdiction over it? But that made no sense. The funeral Mass was to be at St. Raphael's, here on the South Side. Riehle's puzzlement delayed his fear that Father Dowling might recognize him. There was no reason why he should, of course. Marcus Riehle had never spoken with his pastor. For that matter, he was not a registered member of St. Hilary's or of any other parish. He contributed, it wasn't that; he had just not taken the trouble to go to the parish house, put his name on the books, and receive his box of collection envelopes. If the priest would not recognize him, would he recognize his name? That was equally doubtful. Marcus Riehle had learned how anonymous the writer is, no matter that he writes under his own name. People do not associate someone they see every day with a name on a cover, whether of a book or a pamphlet. His own experience was limited to pamphlets, of course. That was why he could remain so invisible and unrecognizable to someone like Mrs. Ennis. To Mrs. Murkin he was visible enough, but not seen for what he really was.

Marcus Riehle turned in his chair and cast an apprehensive look into the lobby behind him. The thought of Mrs. Murkin had brought the fear that she might have accompanied Father Dowling to this wake. But there was no sign of her, and Riehle was relieved. Twice in the past month she had crept up the winding stair to the choir loft and stared with disturbing intensity at Marcus Riehle, who was, as was his wont, filling his soul with the sight and sound of Mrs. Ennis singing her full-bosomed best with the sopranos of the choir.

"There are seats downstairs," she had said to him last

Sunday, coming to stand beside him, her bearing having something of the menace of a cop's.

Marcus Riehle had shaken his head.

"This stairway has to be kept clear."

Riehle considered himself an expert on that stairway, having attended Mass for well over a year standing on it where he could view the choir, or at least the soprano section of it. He shrugged by way of reply. He tried to ignore Mrs. Murkin. He closed his eyes and moved his lips as though in prayer.

"Is something wrong with you?" Mrs. Murkin asked into his darkness.

Riehle was suddenly furious. Who was this busybody to come up the stairway to the choir expressly to harass him? He opened his eyes and glared at her, but when he spoke, it was in a hoarse whisper. The words did not stick in his throat.

"Who do you think you are?"

She drew herself up to her full height of five feet and several-odd inches. "I am the parish housekeeper."

"Big deal." The old phrase, forgotten, he would have thought, came out easily, despite the lethal labial. His anger increased hers.

"What is the matter with you?"

He leaned toward her, breathing from his open mouth. "F-f-f-flu," he said.

She stepped back quickly and went down the stairs, looking back at him with more disgust than anger. There was a lot of Asian flu going around Fox River. Marcus Riehle did not have it. But his claim had the double advantage of getting rid of Mrs. Murkin and providing a plausible explanation of why he was hearing Mass in that unlikely location on the choir stairway. Mrs. Ennis, he was not surprised to notice, had been completely unaware of the little drama unfolding within eyesight of her. That night Marcus Riehle again included Marie Murkin in the prayer he said for his enemies.

It would thus have been perfectly conceivable that a pest like Mrs. Murkin would show up at Enoch Hingle's wake and obstruct Riehle's effort to gather the data he needed for his projected novel. That she was not there suggested he had indeed turned a corner in his career, and perhaps in his life as well. Could Mrs. Ennis ignore a novelist as she did a pamphleteer? Unlikely. Sympathy as well as the instinct for research drew him toward the front of the room after Dowling had finished saying the rosary. When he took the woman's hand, he looked into her red and wary eyes and saw there an imagined mourner at his own wake. His funeral would now be that of a literary man. Crowds of the readers he had pleased and instructed would fill the church, and this weeping woman would be multiplied by thousands.

"The weather could not keep me away as it has the others," he whispered to her. "I am . . ."

He stopped. No need to press his luck. He did not want to stutter here by the body of Enoch Hingle and destroy the scene. For it was a scene he was acting, a rehearsal for the novel. Besides, what he had already said seemed to console the woman. Marcus Riehle turned and walked swiftly from the room.

Father Dowling said the funeral Mass the following day. There were several dozen people in the church beside the mourners of Enoch Hingle. Riehle guessed they were the usual batch of daily Mass goers, there for funerals and weddings when these occurred at the hour they were accustomed to come to church. The weather had turned colder, with a sharp wind coming from the direction of the lake, an overcast sky threatening yet more snow. Marcus Riehle gave his aesthetic approval to the weather. It was precisely as he would have wished it. What he did not approve of, aesthetically or religiously, was the Mass.

The occasion demanded the Requiem Mass of Riehle's childhood, black vestments, the mournful frightening *Dies Irae* and the heart-rending *Agnus Dei*. He thought he detected in Dowling's manner a similar discontent with this new liturgy. In any case, in his novel, the Mass would be a Requiem, no matter Vatican II. How many readers would recognize the anachronism?

When Riehle came out of the church, Mooney recognized him and stepped forward.

"Will you be going to the cemetery, sir?"

Riehle nodded.

"You're welcome to ride in the limousine."

Riehle shook his head, pointing to where his Jeepster was parked. "I have my own c-c-c-...." He let it go. Mooney had understood.

"Are you from the press, sir?"

For answer, Riehle adopted a wise expression. "I'm a writer, yes," he admitted in a whisper. As he walked to his car, he imagined the wondering admiring gaze of Mooney following him.

He followed the procession—if a hearse and a single limousine could be called a procession—to the cemetery. The roads, after they had passed through the stone gateway, were lined with banks of snow, and gravestones wore caps of fluffy white that somehow gave them a sadder aspect, a clownish but ineffectual nosethumbing at death that only emphasized the grim significance of these snow-covered acres. The road branched off just before the open grave and Riehle came to a stop; then, seeing that the hearse had stopped fifty yards farther on, took the road to the left and drove to a point where he could watch the final rites without drawing attention to himself.

Father Dowling got out of the limousine and, accompanied by the woman—Hingle's sister, Riehle had concluded after perusing the brief obituary in the *Tribune*—who was supported by the two Mooneys who had already carried the casket to the site, crossed the snow to where phony grass was draped over the mounds of dirt that had been dug from the cruel earth. (Phrases of a literarily useful sort formed facilely in Marcus Riehle's mind and his sense that he was engaged in a predestined effort increased.) Another car appeared and came to a stop behind the limousine. Riehle had rolled down his window and his memory recorded the crisp complaint of the snow beneath the tires of the car and then the moment of stillness before there was the sound of the door opening. A large man got out of the car and when he slammed the door the sound seemed to flee across the snow-covered graves until it lost itself over the horizon. The man went quickly across the snow to the open grave and assumed a reverent stance.

Riehle eased open his own door and stepped out of the Jeepster. The area between the road on which he had parked and that where the hearse stood seemed particularly deep with snow. He tested it and, misled by the shallow snow beside the road, started across it toward the sad scene of the gravesite. Within four steps the snow was higher than his boots and he decided to stop by a pin oak tree, several of whose leaves lay atop the snow in a confusion of seasons. Riehle leaned his shoulder against the tree and, holding his breath, strained to hear the words Father Dowling was reading from a book, but all he could make out was the measured cadence of the priest's voice. The thin, ascetic-looking pastor of St. Hilary's was, Riehle decided, ideal for this role. He was reminded of Gustave Doré illustrations of *The Divine Comedy*. All Dowling lacked was a Dantesque laurel to complete the illusion that, as he stood beside the grave, he was looking down into the nether world with a ghostly Virgil at his side.

It would have been difficult not to become lost in

thought, standing there that bitter February day in a snow-covered cemetery, leaning against the gnarled trunk of a tree, seeing from a distance the consignment to earth of the mortal remains of Enoch Hingle. But Riehle's thoughts were now less on the project of his novel than on the somber reality of the event. It was not imaginary, his own inevitable death, and whatever pathos might be noticed and enjoyed in so lonely an end for a human being, Marcus Riehle could not ignore the fact that, should he die today or any day before the hoped-for fame that would come as a result of his still unwritten novel, his funeral would be every bit as bleak as Enoch Hingle's. And who could find in his life the failure of promise that had attracted him in Enoch Hingle's bloody end?

He was rescued from melancholy by the sound of the woman's sobbing. Her shoulders were shaking now and Father Dowling extended a small glittering object to her. He meant for her to sprinkle the casket with holy water. When she did take the sprinkler, she shook it only once and Riehle could actually see the spray of water. This marked the end of the graveside ceremony. Riehle pushed away from the tree and turned.

That was when he saw the man standing beside his Jeepster.

19

KEEGAN took the sprinkler from Mrs. Ludwig and shook it vigorously over the casket, conscious of the fact that many would think it ironic that a man whose profession it was to track down the wayward and bring them to justice should by this gesture call down the divine mercy on Enoch Hingle. He said something to this effect to Roger Dowling as they headed back to the road, picking their way among the footprints they had made on the way to the grave.

"Was Enoch Hingle a criminal?" Dowling spoke low so Mrs. Ludwig would not hear him.

Keegan frowned. At headquarters now such a question was answered with another: Does Dolly Parton sleep on her stomach? But he could scarcely use that way of indicating to Roger Dowling the naiveté of his question. "Look at the way he died, Roger."

"That makes him a victim rather than a criminal. What have you learned about all his lost years?"

Keegan nodded toward Mrs. Ludwig. "We have to have a long talk with her."

"She really doesn't know much, Phil."

"Oh?"

"It seems her brother had been living right here in Chicago. Under any number of aliases. They got together from time to time. Last Thanksgiving, for instance."

Keegan made a face. "You found all that out in the line of duty, of course."

"It wasn't just duty, Phil. Who is that with Cy Horvath?"

Mrs. Ludwig had already gotten into the limousine and the door had been closed behind her. Young Mooney turned to face the priest, but now his gaze was drawn toward Horvath and a pudgy man who seemed to be struggling some distance beyond the road. Keegan broke into a run, heading toward Horvath. The little fat man was the one F. X. Mooney had reported, Keegan was sure of it. Horvath looked at Keegan when he came up and the lieutenant's face wore an embarrassed expression. The fat man was apoplectic, sputtering, enraged, but no words came from his mouth. Keegan realized the man was stuttering.

"Give me your identification," Keegan demanded. This man was no one he knew. Despite the temperature, he was sweating profusely.

"N-n-n-n . . ."

Keegan took him by the shoulders, spun him around, and pinned him to the tree. "Check his ID," he ordered Horvath.

It was not the approved method, but Cy fished the

man's wallet out of his left back pocket and opened it. His eyebrows lifted. "Fox River, Illinois. Marcus Riehle."

Keegan spoke over Riehle's shoulder. "You're under arrest. Suspicion of accomplice to a crime. How well did you . . ." He began over. "Did you know Enoch Hingle? Were you friends?"

A moment of nothing, then the man shook his head. Negative.

"Okay. You went to his wake. You went to his funeral. You even came out here for the burial. Enoch Hingle was shot to death in Fox River three days ago. You're under arrest. Take him to the car, Cy."

Keegan went back to where Father Dowling stood in the middle of the road. "What was that all about?"

"His name is Marcus Riehle, Roger. He's from Fox River. Cy will take him in."

"Fox River! Did you recognize him?"

"Never saw him before. Never heard the name either. Chances are he's just one of those freaks who gather like vultures at the scene of a tragedy."

"Or a sports fan, Phil. He could be an old admirer of Enoch Hingle, the star athlete."

Keegan let that go by. "I can drive you back to Fox River, Roger."

"I left my car at Saint Raphael's. Mr. Mooney has offered to take me there."

"Where is Saint Raphael's?"

"I'd better go with Mooney. You have work to do." Roger looked past him, at Horvath, who was leading Riehle to the car he had parked behind the Jeepster.

"Okay, Roger. Maybe I'll see you tonight."

"Good."

Keegan watched the priest get into the front seat, next

to Mooney. The hearse had already departed. Soon the limousine moved soundlessly away. Keegan turned to rejoin Horvath in what suddenly seemed a waste of time, and probably a mistake as well.

"Maybe he's a deaf mute," Cy Horvath suggested three hours later.

"Hasn't he said anything yet?"

Cy shook his head. There was nothing accusing in Horvath's expression, but then, his expression never indicated what he really felt. But Keegan was sure that Horvath, like Roger Dowling, considered it a mistake to bring in Marcus Riehle. He was damned sure Cy had not enjoyed the long drive home at the wheel of Riehle's Jeepster. Hoping to salvage something from the detention of Riehle, Keegan said, "Check out where he lives, Cy. Get a warrant and go out there."

"You want me to lock him up?"

Keegan hesitated. Why compound it if it was a mistake? "Put him in the squad room and have someone keep an eye on him. And have them get a doctor to see if he is a mute."

"I left the Liberati stuff on your desk."

"Anything there?"

"It's hard to say."

That too seemed a rebuke. But then Keegan remembered the bodies of Enoch Hingle and Stevie O'Brien and shrugged away his misgivings. By God, he was going to find out who had killed those two no matter how much of a risk of a false-arrest suit he ran. Nothing in this case was likely to be settled without running risks.

The file on Liberati was about what Keegan thought it would be. A whole list of complaints about the Liberati marina, arrests made there for brawling, for possession, the usual sort of thing for that sort of place. Was Liberati, or someone who worked for him at the marina, a supplier? The question had been raised a number of times but no formal charge had ever been made, no arrests. Liberati had been arrested a number of times for fighting, and there had been two complaints from women who claimed he had abused them. But, as was usual with such complaints, they came from women with whom Liberati was carrying on, and as soon as the police began to look into the matter, a reconciliation took place and the woman became indignant at the police for prying into her private life. One of the women had been visibly bruised, both her eyes blackened. If she hadn't been mauled by Liberati, then it had been by someone else. The assumption was that Liberati was the gallant who had beaten her up. Obviously the man had a terrible temper.

Liberati, Roberto Angelo, born 1942, son of Anna and Carlo Liberati, who had come to this country from Catania in 1937. No brothers or sisters. The complaints about the marina had increased since the death of Anna Liberati in 1963. Those involving young Liberati personally had taken place prior to 1975. Roberto had never married but, for whatever reason, 1975 marked the end of his skirmishes with the police. No charges, no convictions. Although he had been arrested a number of times, swept up in a mass arrest at a beach rumble, he had never been charged.

His interest in pistol meets dated from his school days. Horvath had found this out when he talked with Liberati before he had been bailed out by Tuttle. Contrary to his attorney's advice, he had talked freely with Cy. Most people did, unless they had something to hide. Didn't Liberati have something to hide?

"Everybody has something to hide," Horvath said, sounding like Roger Dowling at his most philosophical.

"Most people don't have two murdered people linked to them the way Enoch Hingle and Stevie O'Brien are linked with Liberati."

"He swears he never heard Hingle's name. I showed him pictures. He says no. He never saw the man before."

"What do his salesmen say?"

"I haven't asked them."

"Hasn't the court appointed an attorney for them yet?"

"Sure. Cornie Ryan. He has advised them not to cooperate until he has a chance to sit down with each of them separately and find out what the hell is going on. Ryan is a very busy man."

"We're lucky it wasn't Tuttle."

"They refused him."

"That's right. Well, by God, we know they're crooks. If they're not connected with Hingle's murder, we can deliver them over to any number of departments that want them."

After Horvath left to check out Marcus Riehle's apartment, Keegan turned his chair toward the window, lit a cigar, and thought of Stevie O'Brien. Iggie was acting as if he hadn't spent a day on the force, demanding that the goddamn police get off their duffs and do something, catch the maniac who had killed his son. How could you explain to a man who already knew it that you don't just snap your fingers and come up with a killer? When Iggie found out they were looking into Stevie's associations and activities, he actually threatened to sue the department. Keegan doubted that he really meant that. He hoped he didn't. What would be gained by forcing them to make public what they had learned about Stevie? Keegan had talked discreetly about that with Martin, the O'Brien son who was in law school.

"Stevie? Come on, Captain Keegan. Stevie was just not that kind of kid."

"They never are, Martin. We hear that day after day. No one's brother or son is ever involved with drugs. As a user, let alone as a pusher."

"We would have known, Keegan. He couldn't have kept that a secret from his own family."

But even as Martin said it, he seemed to be having doubts whether it was true, and well he might have. Maybe a drunk has difficulty keeping his vice a secret from his family and friends, but people on pot and cocaine seemed capable of concealing their habits even from people very closely connected with them in their daily lives. Parents were notoriously fooled by their kids in this as in other matters.

Keegan was glad to see that Martin did not remain on the level of indignation. The young man might very well have been in business with his brother. Stevie's mode of operating might have been learned from the older brother, a family tradition of sorts, grafted onto the father's dream of having his own business. The Owlize patrol cars cruising the city in the small hours, making their deliveries while they checked on the property of Iggie's clients: it was a very smooth operation.

"You're taking the word of addicts about this, Captain?"

"Two pounds of marijuana and several ounces of cocaine were found in the patrol car your brother was driving."

"My God! What did my father say to that?"

Keegan looked Martin directly in the eye. "I haven't told him. And I don't intend to tell him unless I have to. You had no idea your brother was engaged in this sort of thing?"

Martin shook his head, a faraway look in his eye. "No." Keegan wondered if Martin would mourn his brother less now that he knew the way Stevie had exploited their father's business. "Was Jack—"

"Apparently not."

"You questioned him?"

"We checked out all the Owlize vehicles. There is no

trace or indication that they were used in the same way. Stevie always drove the same Volkswagen."

"That's right. Number three."

"I suppose the customers recognized him by the number."

"Please don't tell my parents, Captain. It would kill them. And what good would be served?"

"I hope I don't have to, Martin."

When the young man left, he carried with him the burden of his brother's secret guilt. Martin looked ready to bear the family's shame in silence and alone, and Keegan liked him for it. Martin reminded him of Iggie in the old days, when Iggie was still a cop.

20

THEY WEREN'T his parishioners but they were Phil Keegan's friends, so when Phil asked Father Dowling to go talk with Sally and Iggie O'Brien, the priest went.

"He was on the force, Roger. He was a good cop." Keegam said this as if exonerating O'Brien of some fault. "He should never have left." That, apparently, was the fault.

"How are they taking it?"

"Bad. Mainly Iggie. But Sally has been lying in a darkened room with a washcloth over her eyes. They need a priest."

Well, they needed what a priest represented: the faith that what makes no sense to us somehow makes sense after all. What was that line from Eliot, summarizing human life? "Birth, copulation, and death." The poet might have been sketching the main concerns of the priest. Baptism, confession, funerals.

Standing on the stoop of the O'Brien home, waiting for his ring to be answered, Roger Dowling felt like a salesman representing an unwanted product. But then the door opened and a thickset disheveled man looked out at him, saw the Roman collar, and stepped back for Roger Dowling to enter.

"I'm Father Dowling. A friend of Phil Keegan's."

O'Brien nodded as if he had lost all capacity for surprise. Dowling caught the scent of whiskey when he passed the man. Apparently he was keeping a solitary Irish wake. A young man rose from a chair when Dowling came into the living room but, unlike Iggie O'Brien, his response to the arrival of a priest was less automatic. Father Dowling told the young man who he was.

"I'm Martin. Martin O'Brien."

Ah yes. The son. Part of the family enterprise, now a student of the law. Martin's expression remained half resentful. "I made arrangements with Monsignor Hogan."

Dowling nodded. Hogan was pastor of Sacred Heart, a good man if somewhat querulous about the ravages wrought by Vatican II. Hogan had bet Dowling they would both live to see Martin Luther declared a Doctor of the Church.

Iggie O'Brien said, "My wife won't come out, Father. She is beyond consolation."

"She won't even take a drink," Martin said. His voice was even, not quite an accusation.

Roger Dowling turned to the father. "Where is she?"
"In her room."

"Would it help if I went to her?"

"Would you do that, Father?"

Martin O'Brien showed him the way, leading him out of the living room, down a hallway to the stairs. He went up ahead of the priest but stopped on the landing and turned.

"You realize my brother was murdered?"

"Yes."

"We haven't given her the details. All she knows is that he is dead."

The young man looked at Dowling as if he expected this to be challenged.

"Have you any notion who might have done it?"

"What does it matter? My father seems to think it would be a solution if the murderer were caught."

"Don't you?"

"I am only months from finishing law school. I know what a lawyer can do in such cases."

Dowling nodded. "I see what you mean. But think of the poor devil who did it. Imagine running around free with something like that on your conscience."

"I doubt that he has one."

"A conscience? Oh, we all do."

Martin stopped himself from saying something. Perhaps it was just as well. Martin O'Brien seemed cynical and bitter. Well, his younger brother was dead. No doubt the world had taken on a different and bitter look to him now. This wasn't the moment to address his resentment, but Father Dowling made a mental note to have a talk with Martin before bitterness settled more deeply into his soul. But Martin had turned and continued up the stairs. At the closed door of a room, he stopped and tapped softly.

"Mom? Mom, there's someone here to see you. A priest."

His voice had become a boy's voice. There was a murmur from within and Martin pushed open the door and indicated to Father Dowling that he could enter.

The priest stood at the door of the darkened bedroom, waiting for his eyes to adjust. Martin went back downstairs. Light shown dimly at the edges of the drawn shades; tied-back curtains became visible; from the darkness came a woman's sob. Roger Dowling hoped she would turn on a light.

"Monsignor Hogan?"

The grieving woman's voice sounded generic, a blend of Enoch Hingle's sister's and a hundred others Roger Dowling had heard over the years. The springs of the bed creaked, there was the sound of sighing exertion and a small lamp with a pink ribbed shade was lighted. In its friendly glow Mrs. O'Brien became visible, her hair a mess, eyes puffy with tears. She looked startled when she looked at her visitor.

"I'm Father Dowling. From Saint Hilary's. Phil Keegan asked me to stop by."

She pushed herself into a sitting position and a hand went to her hair momentarily. She let it drop. She was beyond vanity now. Her son was dead. Father Dowling went into the room and pulled a small chair with a half back out from the dressing table and sat.

"You're a friend of Captain Keegan's?"

"Yes."

"It was good of you to come. Have you talked with Iggie? My husband."

"He's doing fine."

"He's drinking."

"Martin's with him."

The reminder of a surviving son released her tears. Roger Dowling realized she was holding a photograph of a boy. Stevie? Most likely. She pressed it to her and rocked on the bed, weeping without shame. And talked.

She had not realized that her son's job was dangerous. She had been happy he was not on the regular police force like his father. For years she had lived in dread that something would happen to Iggie. She had never had such fears for Stevie. And now Stevie was dead. Shot. So they had told her that much. Well, what else did she have to know now? Eventually, she would learn the rest. They would not be able to keep from his mother how Stevie had got into trouble. When she subsided and only cried, Father Dowling knelt on the floor and suggested they pray.

He said a decade of the rosary and she joined in and he prayed that she would see life as it really is, lived in the continuous presence of God Almighty. This bedroom in a middle-class home where a mother wept for her dead son did not escape the all-encompassing eye of God. He was with her now. He understood a mother's grief. When they finished the prayers, he told her this, matter-of-factly, telling her truths she already knew but had to realize now. And then they prayed again, for the repose of Stevie's soul.

"He was a good boy, Father. Such a good boy."

Well, good as men are good, but God is even more merciful than a doting parent. When Father Dowling stood, Mrs. O'Brien got off the bed.

"I'll put on some coffee," she said. "You go down. I'll be there in a minute." She put her hand on his arm. "Thank you, Father."

She was crying again when he left the room and went down the stairs. There was much crying yet that she must do.

In the living room, Iggie O'Brien sat on the middle cushion of the couch, the glass he held resting on his knee. He looked up at Roger Dowling with imperfectly focused eyes.

"Where's Martin?"

"Gone. How's Sally?"

"She's coming down."

"Can I offer you a drink, Father?"

"No thank you. Your wife is going to make coffee."

"I'll make it." He tried to rise from the couch, bending

forward, attempting to rise to his feet. His drink sloshed in his glass.

"Let her do it. She wants to. That will be best."

Iggie O'Brien nodded sagely, pursing his lips and sharing a look with the priest. Roger Dowling might have just uttered a truism about the female sex in mourning.

"Getting her out of that room is a triumph, Father. *I* couldn't do it. This is hard on her, hard." He took several rapid breaths, and his mouth trembled, but he gained control of himself. Why should he want to be so stoic? Had he wept for his son yet?

"What happened to Stevie?" Roger Dowling asked.

"He was shot!"

"By whom?"

Iggie O'Brien glared at him. "Read the papers, Father. The world is populated by maniacs. Junkies, thrill-seekers, madmen. They kill without a thought. There doesn't have to be a reason. They just kill people." He brought his glass to his lips and drank, glaring at Roger Dowling as he did so. "And society is blamed."

From the kitchen came the sound of water running. Mrs. O'Brien making coffee.

"Your wife said she thought his job was a safe one."

"It was! Nothing like this ever happened before. I don't mean I'm surprised. I was a cop for years. I know this town."

"What do you mean?"

O'Brien's eyes narrowed in knowledgeability. "Do you know what a city looks like to a cop? A zoo! You see our neighborhoods and you might think all those families are nice as pie. Downtown is full of upright businessmen, right? Everybody stops for traffic lights, everyone pays his taxes. Civilization." O'Brien spoke the word with contempt. "Well, a cop runs into upright citizens in the strangest situations. Bankers, workers, nice kids. Priests. When the sun goes down the animals come out of their cages. That's why there's a market for Owlize. I run a private security firm. You don't stamp out crime, Father. You control it. The police know all kinds of crooks they can't arrest because they are too careful. What do you know of Liberati?"

"The man whose truck was stolen?"

"The family. Family! That's the word for them. They are the mob in Fox River, Father."

"Your client?"

"I mean the family."

"You're full of sauce, Iggie." Mrs. O'Brien had come into the room. She had washed her face and her hair was tidy, but her tear-reddened eyes looked gently at her husband. "Coffee's on."

"I don't want any," Iggie growled.

"Yes, you do."

"Are you suggesting that Liberati is involved in your son's death?"

Roger Dowling's question angered Iggie. He scowled at the priest, his eyes darting to his wife.

"I'll leave that to Phil Keegan," Iggie O'Brien said.

When he went out to his car, Roger Dowling looked up and down the wide winding suburban street on which the O'Briens lived. Was this part of the zoo Iggie had raged about? Of course it was. Did O'Brien think a priest was unaware of the fragility of men? Cops and clergy exist because of that shared weakness winding back through history to a defiant choice in a garden. Original sin. The Vale of Tears. Roger Dowling knew all about that, and not simply from observing others.

Iggie O'Brien's reaction was familiar. When we have done something wrong, we point to another whose sins are darker than our own. Iggie O'Brien could look past his son's wrongdoing by pointing at the Liberatis. The Liberatis. Was the old man who spent his days at St. Hilary's Center part of that family?

Dusk was gathering when he got back to his parish. Cars of those who had come to pick up old people who had spent the day at the Center clogged the street and Father Dowling pulled over to the curb to wait until the congestion cleared. He might have left his car there and walked to the rectory, but he decided not to. His decision was made when he saw old Carlo Liberati coming along the sidewalk from the school. Old? He looked dapper and full of energy and he walked at a brisk pace. As he approached the car ahead of Father Dowling, his eyes crinkled and he fluttered the gloved fingers of one hand. The woman at the wheel leaned across the seat and unlocked the door. She did not fully resume her seated position while Carlo got in. He gave her a kiss. The woman was a good deal younger than Carlo, a brassy blonde. His daughter? Not likely.

Roger Dowling put his car in gear and eased into the street. When he was alongside the other car, he turned and took a careful look at the blonde woman and Carlo Liberati. They did not notice him. They were talking in a faintly uxorial way. Had the old man married again? Roger Dowling resolved to find out more from Edna Hospers about Carlo Liberati.

21

Cy Horvath did not like the way the investigation was going. He didn't like it at all.

Take Marcus Riehle. Please. So the guy had gone to Hingle's wake and funeral, so he had gone on to the cemetery for the burial. Was that a crime? Riehle had tried to talk at first and been unable to; now he was keeping silent on principle. They had let him go, of course, but not until the embarrassment of the search of Riehle's apartment and the ridiculous testimony or whatever you wanted to call it of Mrs. Murkin and Mrs. Ennis.

"Ennis?" Keegan had said. "Who the hell is she?"

"She sings in the Saint Hilary choir."

"So what?"

"Mrs. Murkin brought her."

"Marie Murkin is here?"

Keegan seemed almost delighted by the housekeeper's visit. At first. He asked Horvath to stick around and the lieutenant saw how Keegan froze up once Mrs. Murkin got going.

"I think I have solved the mystery, Captain Keegan. This is Mrs. Ennis."

"I understand she sings in the choir," Keegan said, nodding perfunctorily at the object of this remark.

Mrs. Ennis giggled and looked askance at Keegan. "Well, I hardly want my life summed up in quite that way, Captain Keegan. I do one or two other things as well."

Keegan seemed ready to listen to an enumeration of all the things that occupied the day of Mrs. Ennis, probably to get as far away as he could from Mrs. Murkin's opening remark. Keegan might be happy enough to talk over cases with Father Dowling, and he was the first to admit that the pastor of St. Hilary's had often been of decisive help in resolving a case, but Horvath doubted that Keegan would extend this tolerance for amateur help to the housekeeper of St. Hilary's rectory as well.

"It's this creature Marcus Riehle," Mrs. Murkin said, slipping to the edge of the chair Keegan had put her in. "He has been prowling around Saint Hilary's, spying on Mrs. Ennis in the choir loft. . . ."

Horvath leaned back against the wall and closed his eyes, remembering the studio apartment he had gone through in less than thorough fashion. Except for the file cabinets and the pasteboard cartons, the place was furnished basically with a bed and a desk. The only chair in the room was drawn up to the desk. It was pretty clear that Marcus Riehle lived his life at his typewriter. The file cabinets were filled with what Horvath took to be manuscripts, the pasteboard boxes were filled with the kind of pamphlets you used to see in the rear of churches, still did see at the rear of St. Hilary's. Cy took several pamphlets, randomly selected. There was no trace in the room of any interest in Enoch Hingle. There wasn't even a television set, an indispensable instrument for the sports enthusiast. Imagine someone living in this country today who did not watch television. Keegan, when he saw them, was as puzzled by the pamphlets as Horvath had been. He put them away in a drawer of his desk.

"Let him go," he said without looking up.

Horvath let Riehle go. Would he sue them? He had every right to. They should never have allowed themselves to be guided by a nervous mortician. Mooney seemed to think he had a mass-murderer hanging around his establishment. And now Marie Murkin, of all people, was pointing the finger at Marcus Riehle.

"Marie," Keegan said, "just what mystery is cleared up when we know that Marcus Riehle makes goo-goo eyes at Mrs. Ennis when she is singing in the choir during the ten-thirty Mass every Sunday at Saint Hilary's?"

"There is more. Tell him, Martha."

Mrs. Ennis, flustered, looked from Marie to Keegan and back again. Finally she unsnapped a purse the size of a saddle bag, pulled out a letter, and slapped it on Keegan's desk. Horvath crossed the room and stood beside Keegan when he unfolded the single page. The typing looked similar to that of Riehle's machine. It was a species of love letter, expressing respect and admiration for Mrs. Ennis's work with the Fox River writers and shyly hinting at more.

"It isn't signed Marcus Riehle," Keegan observed.

It was Marie Murkin's turn to pull something from her purse. It was one of the pamphlets Horvath had confiscated from Riehle's apartment. She got up, put her purse on the chair, and came around the desk so that she and Horvath were flanking the seated Keegan. Mrs. Ennis, clasping her purse in both hands, leaned forward attentively.

Mrs. Murkin opened the pamphlet, laid it before Keegan, and pointed. "There. 'To M.E.'"

"Oh, Mrs. Murkin," Mrs. Ennis cried in a little squeal. "That could be anyone."

"It is you, Martha, and you know it. Mar-tha En-nis," Mrs. Murkin said; she might have been spelling the words. "There is your connection, Captain Keegan."

Mrs. Murkin marched around the desk and resumed her seat.

"Captain Keegan," she continued, "as you know, I often know more than I should about the work you are engaged in and we needn't go into that. It is safe to make the point within these walls. Very well. I know of the suspicions that have been directed at this Riehle person. I have heard about the wake and funeral and all the rest. Obviously you already have a strong case against him. I offer you this information to make it stronger. Let me tell you a little story. . . ."

Horvath left in the midst of the anecdote concerning Riehle's deliberately and insultingly blowing flu germs at Mrs. Murkin when she confronted him on the choir stairway. Before going, he scribbled "Liberati" on a slip of paper and put it by Keegan's elbow. Before he closed the door, Keegan called after him.

"No warrant, Cy. You know why."

Horvath nodded and closed the door.

It seemed crazy that they should be wasting their time with someone like Marcus Riehle and with informants like Mrs. Murkin and Mrs. Ennis, when Liberati, whose salesmen almost certainly were involved in the death of Enoch Hingle, was out on bond and no longer willing to say a word. So what they needed was a warrant, to look into Liberati's business operations, both at the used-car lot and at the marina as well. That was a perfectly reasonable request, given the character of his sales personnel, indeed it was an absolutely necessary and obvious one; but it was a request they could not make. Robertson. Horvath had been hauled in with Keegan for a little lecture on civil rights laced with allusions to Fox River politics.

"The man has a clear case of police harassment against us as it is. You run him in like some kind of common hoodlum after already having questioned him in what he characterizes as an insolent manner about some stolen property. Then you actually arrest him on suspicion of murder. Murder! What conceivable connection is there between Liberati and the death of Enoch Hingle?"

"The weapon," Keegan said. The muscles in the captain's jaw were working.

Robertson consulted a paper on his desk. "A .22 pistol. Have you found the weapon?"

"No, sir."

"You do not have in your possession what you claim is the link between Liberati and the dead man?"

Horvath said, "The truck in which Enoch Hingle's body was found had been stolen from Liberati's lot. For some reason, he never reported the theft, either to the police or to the private security people he employs. The truck in which the body was found had been towed to Saint Hilary's. It was almost certainly towed by another Liberati vehicle. That second vehicle has fingerprints of Liberati's sales force all over it. The sales force is as much of a connection as the weapon."

"What about the first truck?"

"Sir?"

"Are the fingerprints of these men in that truck?"

"No, sir."

Robertson fell back in his chair. "Well, then, for the love of God . . ."

"That's just the point," Keegan said. "Why aren't their prints in that truck? Cy had a random check made of vehicles in the lot and the fingerprints of one or more of those men were found in them. There are no prints at all in the stolen truck. It was wiped."

"And that is your basis for arresting Liberati?"

"That is why we arrested the three men." Keegan paused and, when he went on, he was making a visible effort to keep his tone factual and neutral. "They worked for Liberati. What we have going here, Chief, is some kind of struggle among drug traffickers. The three salesmen are hirelings; they're not in charge of anything."

"They are also innocent of the death of the O'Brien boy," Robertson said, his tone one of sweet reasonableness. "Look, Captain, Lieutenant, I know what you're thinking. You think I am acting out of political considerations alone. I will not pretend that I am unconscious of the political ramifications, but for God's sake, think about it. Even if there is some sort of mob struggle going on here, what has that to do with Liberati? Are you suggesting that a member of that family is in league with the underworld?"

There was a long pause and Horvath wondered if Keegan would lay out the whole network of conjecture for Robertson. He was mightily relieved when Keegan did not.

"Chief, all I ask is freedom to investigate. If Liberati is innocent, that will be proved and he will benefit from it."

"Keegan, the assumption has to be that he *is* innocent."

There was more; with Robertson there was always more. He did not like instructing Keegan on how to do his job. And he wanted not only compliance, but agreement; he spent half an hour not getting that. The upshot of the meeting was that no warrants or subpoenas were to be issued that would permit them to look at Liberati's books, search the premises of the used-car lot or the office at the marina.

And that is why Horvath made the pointless search of Marcus Riehle's apartment and Keegan was even now wasting his time listening to Mrs. Murkin and Mrs. Ennis. Horvath might not have a warrant to search Liberati's office, but he sure as hell had the right to make a social call. It had struck him that Charmaine might be as informative as any search warrant would permit, particularly because of what had seemed her sincere shock at the death of Stevie O'Brien.

On the way to the used-car lot, Horvath decided to stop by McDivitt's where Stevie O'Brien was being waked.

Martin O'Brien was more or less in charge of things, McDivitt told Horvath, his pale manicured hand fluttering over the cottony hair that seemed whiter because of his florid complexion and the black suit he wore.

"The mother is inconsolable, of course. And the father, well . . ."

Iggie O'Brien had always been an excitable man, Horvath considered. Although O'Brien had been a sergeant when Horvath was a rookie and they had never been close, that kind of distance made for a more objective and disinterested appraisal. In those days, Horvath had been unconsciously seeking the model of the kind of cop he wanted to be and he had not yet recognized that his model would be Phil Keegan. O'Brien he had discarded within days. Not that the man did not have his merits. He was diligent and loyal—you would never have worried about being in a car with him if trouble broke out—and generally he went by the book. But there was a point too easily reached when his emotional involvement in a case caused his zeal to run away with him. Oddly enough, one such occasion had involved the Liberati marina.

Iggie had become convinced there had to be some connection between Carlo Liberati and the repeated instances of drug-related disturbances at the marina. He had actually used one of his own sons as a decoy, without authorization. Martin had made a purchase and then had been picked up in a raid and poor Iggie was caught trying to extricate his son with his story of a free-lance investigation. Undeniably the kid had been picked up with a dozen reefers in his possession. Phil Keegan had backed up O'Brien, had even let it be thought he had been in on the crazy plan from the beginning, and his already immense authority had gotten Martin O'Brien off without a record. That was when Horvath saw that Keegan was the kind of cop he wanted to be. Particularly after he overheard Keegan chewing O'Brien out in what he had thought was a private conversation. Horvath, at his locker several aisles over, let several minutes go by before clearing his throat and slamming his locker door to let them know he was there. Keegan came and looked at Horvath and that was all. He said nothing to Cy, and when weeks passed and it was obvious that Horvath had kept his mouth shut about what he had overheard, Keegan took on the young cop as his protégé.

How long had it been since he saw Martin O'Brien? Long enough for Horvath to be surprised and not a little intimidated by the tall confident figure in the three-piece suit who came toward him, extending his hand only at the last moment as recognition shone in his eyes.

"Officer Horvath, isn't it?"

"Lieutenant." Martin had not smiled and neither did he. Insisting on his rank seemed a necessity in the circumstances.

"What have they found out?"

About Stevie? More than they had wanted to, more than they wanted to tell Iggie. But Martin, according to Keegan, had taken the bad news reasonably well. Horvath shrugged.

"Whoever framed him is the one who killed him, Lieutenant."

"You may be right."

"You sound skeptical."

"He wasn't framed, Martin."

"Listen, Horvath, I know Stevie. . . ."

He stopped himself. His voice had risen. His eyes went past Horvath into the room beyond. Horvath turned. The casket containing Stevie O'Brien was surrounded by a sea of flowers. Speak well of the dead? In Stevie's case, that would mean saying nothing at all. Well, this was certainly not the place to discuss with Martin why there was no doubt about Stevie's guilt. For the past two nights, an officer had toured Stevie's Owlize route in his Volkswagen and been hailed down by dozens of potential buyers. Even so, Horvath thought it was right that Martin did not believe his brother could be guilty of such a thing.

"How long since you drove an Owlize route, Martin?"

"A law student doesn't have time for anything but law. Why?"

The two men stood looking at each other for a full minute during which Martin got the point of the question. Neither blinked or turned away. They were rescued by the arrival of McDivitt. Even then, Horvath let Martin acknowledge the mortician's presence and turn away first.

Charmaine was typing when he entered the office and she did not turn, although Horvath had deliberately made a bit of noise getting the flimsy door shut again. How could anyone stand to work in a world of aluminum, let alone live in it? Mobile homes are seldom mobile and they aren't much of a home either, or so Horvath thought. He crossed the office to Charmaine's desk and she began to speak without looking at him.

"Your father called."

"I doubt that, Charmaine. He's been dead for three years."

"Oh! I thought you were Rob. Mr. Liberati."

"Maybe I should have phoned first, but I was just in the neighborhood and I thought I'd drop by. Mr. Liberati isn't in?"

"No, he isn't. You were just in the neighborhood the other day too." A little smile played on her full lips. They seemed moist and Horvath decided it must be the stuff she put on them. Or maybe they were chapped.

"I was watching the place that day."

"Whatever for?" She pressed a key on her typewriter, turning it off, and swung in her chair to face him.

"Because funny things have been going on around here lately. From a policeman's point of view, I mean. Tell me about it, Charmaine."

"You remembered my name," she said, pleased. "Yours is what, Bill?"

He showed her his ID, making the visit as legitimate as he could. "You're thinking of Captain Keegan. His name is Philip. Mine is Cyril. People call me Cy. Why didn't Liberati report that stolen truck?"

"Don't you think you should ask him that?" She looked at him playfully, however, as if he were being naughty in a way she didn't really object to.

"I have asked him. He says he simply didn't think of it. He didn't report it to Owlize either. Same reason. I suppose that is plausible enough."

"Well, all I know is that he didn't report it. Not from here anyway, not while I was at work."

"How long have you worked here?"

She sighed, and Horvath had to hold his eyes high so as not to be distracted by her heaving bosom. "Too long, I can tell you that." She looked around the office and sighed again.

"Not much of a job, is it? I mean, there doesn't seem to be much business. How long is too long?"

"Ever since he opened the lot. That was in November. It's not the kind of job I thought it would be. I am a very good secretary. Most of my jobs have been highly responsible ones. Not that I move around a lot, but before I came here I was secretary to the vice-president in charge of management at the Kissey Corporation."

"What do they make, candy?"

She thought about it for a moment, then laughed. "No, they're dry cleaners. A huge company, all over the Chicago metropolitan area. You must have seen the billboards."

"Lips?"

"Right." And she pursed hers in the kissing pose that was the trade mark of the dry cleaner.

"Why did you leave there?"

"My boss." She hesitated, not looking him in the eye, as if inviting him to fill in the blanks. "He got fresh. Too fresh. He seemed to think my job included overtime with him. 'On a personal basis.' His words."

Horvath frowned sympathetically and shook his head.

"Then he got fired, so I left too."

"When do you expect Liberati back?"

"Expect him? I haven't the faintest idea. That is the crazy thing about this job. How can I run things if I don't know where he is or when he'll be coming in?"

Horvath said that sounded tough all right. "Particularly if someone wants to buy a car or truck. Is selling part of your job description?"

"Selling? Let me tell you, if the way business is done here is typical of the used-car business, it is a good way to starve to death."

"Sales are off?"

"Off from what?"

"But Liberati had three salesmen."

She turned her face forty-five degrees and looked at him with one fish eye. "Come on. You knew right away those three weren't salesmen. Not of cars and trucks, anyway."

"Then why did Liberati hire them?" It seemed best to go on playing dumb, though Charmaine seemed to need no artifice of his in order to talk. No doubt it was lonely here now, without Albini and Gruening and DiNigro to kid around with.

"I don't think he had a lot of choice."

"You suspected they were wanted men. Why couldn't Liberati see that?"

She opened the drawer of her desk and brought out a package of filter cigarettes. She shook one free for him but he refused. "You don't mind if I smoke, do you?"

"Of course not."

"He does. Can you imagine? You'd think this was a doctor's office. He even made the salesmen go outside when they wanted a smoke."

"It bothers some people."

She lit a cigarette and tipped back her head to blow smoke at the ceiling. "I ought to quit. There's no future here. Besides, it's not . . ."

Horvath just waited. He didn't know why people opened up like this for him, but they did. It was what he had hoped for when he came here.

"Well," she said. "I guess you have your suspicions or you wouldn't have been in the neighborhood."

Horvath nodded. "Did Stevie O'Brien and Liberati get along?"

"Oh, sure. Everybody got along with Stevie." She stopped. "I can't believe he's dead."

"He's dead. I just came from the funeral home where he's laid out."

"It's McDivitt's, isn't it? I was thinking I should stop by, pay my respects. He was Catholic, wasn't he?"

"The family is."

"Can a Protestant go? Is it allowed?"

"Of course. I think it would be nice. You said you liked Stevie."

"He was cute. That day you were here? What a game. He asked me to pretend I didn't really know him. Know why? His father. He didn't want his father to know we were friends. Isn't that a kick? A man his age."

"He was twenty-one."

"I saw they gave that age in the paper. Wasn't it a mistake? He told me he was twenty-five."

"That's Martin."

"Oh." Apparently she knew who Martin was.

"Did Stevie work for Liberati, Charmaine?"

"For him? You're kidding. He always said that if Rob knew of his sideline there would be hell to pay."

"And there was."

"What do you mean?"

"Hell to pay. Stevie was gunned down. With a .22."

The thought might never have occurred to her before. Was she really that dumb? Horvath began to be uneasy about how smoothly all this was going. He walked in and said hello and in minutes she was telling him she knew the sales force was

○ 168 ○

fake and as much as said her boss was in the drug trade and Stevie O'Brien had been competing with him.

"What about Hingle, Charmaine?"

"Hingle?"

"The man whose body was found in the stolen truck."

She stubbed out her cigarette and looked reproachfully at him. "You must think I'm a regular blabbermouth. You come in here and ask a few questions and just look at me."

"It's a lonely job."

"Yours?"

"I was thinking of yours." He pretended he had not heard the muted invitation in her voice.

"Oh, oh. Speak of the devil. Look who's here."

Horvath turned and saw Liberati getting out of a car that had drawn up at the door of the office. Horvath didn't like the fact that he had not heard the car approach. When Liberati came in, Horvath was on his feet, looking down at Charmaine.

"What the hell are you doing here, Horvath?"

He turned. "Getting the run-around from your secretary. She was just assuring me you wouldn't be back today."

"That's true as far as you're concerned. We have nothing to talk about."

Liberati brushed past Horvath, unlocked the door of his office and went into it, leaving the door open. A moment later he hollered for Charmaine to come in there.

She got up, mouthed her thanks to Horvath, and rhythmically walked into her boss's office. Talking with Charmaine had netted Horvath more than a search warrant ever could have.

If he could believe her.

If anybody could really be that dumb.

22

WHENEVER Cletus Rabb came to visit, Roger Dowling thought of his old friend as being out on parole, and indeed, the chaplain from Joliet seemed to feel the same way himself.

"It's not all that different from a monastery, Roger. Regular life, fully scheduled day, walls around the place."

"A lot of monks would consider that libel."

"Let them. What can they do to a lifer?"

Rabb had steel gray hair that he wore in a modified crew cut and his leathery face was deeply creased. Pale blue eyes looked out from under his thick brows and they were twinkling eyes, compassionate eyes, the eyes of a man who has heard a thousand tragic stories. How odd it was, the jobs one's classmates ended up in. They had one army chaplain recently raised to general's rank; they had their share of hospital chaplains and chaplains to convents of nuns. There were teachers and journalists and fund raisers; there were famous preachers and retreat masters. By and large, however, they were in parish work. Yet almost without exception, each man seemed to be in the job for which he had been destined. Did the others see the pastor of St. Hilary's as finally arrived in his fated harbor? Rabb did.

"I could never see you on that marriage court, Roger. Nor as the auxiliary bishop everone said you were bound to become. My God, the prospect would be enough to drive anyone to drink."

Roger Dowling smiled. One's infirmities were almost badges of rank with someone like Cletus Rabb. The prison chaplain did not wonder whether or not a person had a serious flaw, but rather what the flaw was.

"It wasn't all that simple, Clete."

"Simple? Who said simple? But you belong here, Roger. A broken-down parish for a broken-down canonist." And he punched Roger's arm to take the sting out of the remark. "How is your ex-con doing?"

"Feeney? Just fine. I don't think of him as an ex-con, though."

"Well, that is what he is. No need to pretend otherwise. I hope you're keeping a close eye on him. Lead us not into temptation, you know. The man is weak, as are we all, and you mustn't give him a chance to revert to his old ways. Recidivism, as we call it in the trade. Also known as Original Sin."

"I'll keep an eye on him."

"But he's been keeping his nose clean?"

"As far as I know. I don't keep watch on him."

Why at that particular moment did he have a vivid image of the jimmied coin slot on the pamphlet rack at the back of the church? It was unfair to go scouting through the past weeks for things Feeney might be guilty of. Roger Dowling did not know whether to feel proud or naive because he had never connected Feeney with that theft. Or with the missing pork chops and preserves either. What was really surprising was that Marie Murkin had not suspected Feeney either. She simply did not care for the new janitor and made little effort to hide her feelings. Roger Dowling had warned her about that, to no avail. But the thefts had been eclipsed by the discovery of Enoch Hingle in the abandoned and stolen truck parked at the curb. It was as if both he and Mrs. Murkin had considered the three events to be connected.

"We did have a murder in the neighborhood, Clete. At least, the body was found in a truck parked right out on that street."

"Murder? No. That's not Feeney. Far beyond him, anything that daring."

"You make murder sound courageous."

"Foolhardy, not courageous. But not just anyone can commit murder."

"I'm not so sure."

"Say, how is Phil Keegan anyway?"

"He'll be over later. I thought the three of us could go see a Blackhawks game."

"And I was just getting warm. Got any more of this?"

Rabb was drinking bourbon and water. Roger Dowling took his glass into the kitchen, put fresh cubes in, and uncorked the bottle. He held it under his nose and let the fumes stir the olfactory memories of his years of degradation. The smell was no more enticing to him than, he hoped, the thought of a return to crime was for Feeney. Rabb had a long experience with the criminal mind, but Roger Dowling wondered if he was sufficiently aware of the repulsiveness of sin and weakness to one who has escaped them. He made Rabb's drink of moderate proportions. The reformed alcoholic had to be careful about the size of drinks he served his guests, not make them huge, as if others could not be affected by alcohol as he was and it did not matter how much they drank. As Rabb might have agreed, alcoholism was not like freckles. It was more like a tan, something acquired that turned easily into a sunburn.

"Is Feeney around?" Rabb asked when Roger Dowling returned to the study.

"I told him you were coming."

"That was fair enough. He had a chance to escape."

"More likely than not, he's over at the school. When you finish that, we can stroll over there."

When they did go over to the school and knocked on Feeney's door there was no answer. Perhaps the babble of noise from the old people prevented him from hearing the knock. Rabb tried the door and, to Dowling's surprise, pushed it open and went inside.

"Is he there?" he asked from the hall.

"Not unless he's hiding under the bed."

Roger Dowling waited but Rabb did not come out. He looked into the room and was startled to find Rabb going systematically through the drawers of the dresser. He looked over his shoulder at Roger Dowling. "Don't act so shocked. I won't find anything."

"You shouldn't be looking."

"He expects it," Rabb said enigmatically, and went on with his search.

Somehow Cletus Rabb's manner conferred a kind of legitimacy on what he was doing, though Roger Dowling did not like it. He looked around the little room and thought how little imprint Feeney had made upon it. The room might have been a cell, impersonal, cold, anybody's. How lonely Feeney's life must be. Roger Dowling felt a pang of guilt when he considered how little he had got to know Feeney since he had come to St. Hilary's. The man was so unobtrusive and quiet that Roger Dowling had not thought he was ignoring Feeney. On the contrary. To attempt to engage him in conversation seemed as much of a violation as invading his room like this.

"Well, well," a voice said from the doorway. "Has something happened to Mr. Feeney?"

Roger Dowling turned with a start to face Jennie Carr, who smiled at him in a way he did not like.

"Have you seen him, Jennie?"

"Did you think he was hiding in a dresser drawer?"

Cletus Rabb came across the room with his hand extended. Jennie, momentarily flustered, allowed the strange priest to envelope her small hand in one of his huge ones.

"I am Father Rabb, ma'am. An old friend of Mr. Feeney's. And who might you be?"

Roger Dowling made the introductions, feeling somewhat foolish, but the little ceremony seemed to further legitimize their invasion of Feeney's room. Rabb asked Jennie how well she knew Feeney.

"Know him? Good heavens, I don't know him. Not any more than anyone else does, anyway. *Has* something happened to him?"

"Why would you think that?"

"Well, here the two of you are . . ."

"And you were expecting to find Mr. Feeney?" Rabb's long-toothed smile seemed to invite confidence, but Jennie grew wary.

"The last time I saw him he was heading toward the parish house."

"Then we'll look for him over there, right, Roger?"

They stepped into the hallway and Rabb pulled

Feeney's door closed behind him. Jennie went off down the hallway in the direction of the elderly babble and Roger Dowling and Cletus Rabb stood looking after her.

"Now, there is an odd little lady," Cletus Rabb said.

And it was all Roger Dowling could do not to tell Rabb how very odd she was.

23

FROM HIS hide-out behind the furnace in the basement of the parish house, Feeney had listened to the rumbling voice of Father Rabb in the study above. At first he had tried to make out what the two priests were talking about, but after awhile he gave it up. Sooner or later he would have to come out of hiding and subject himself to a grilling by the chaplain from Joliet. He neither looked forward to nor did he dread it. For three years he had been chaplain's assistant to Rabb and they had gotten along fairly well, even though Rabb knew that Feeney no longer believed anything. Maybe if he had been a lifer without hope, those old thoughts of heaven, of rewards and vindication in the next world, would have had their appeal, but the heaven he looked forward to, or thought he did, lay beyond the unpearly gates of the prison and he was willing to settle for that.

During his last year, when the thought of impending

freedom began to oppress him, he had tried to talk to Rabb about it, but the gruff chaplain assumed he knew more about prison life than the prisoners and refused to take Feeney's apprehensions seriously.

"You'll love it, Tim. And don't worry, you'll go right from here to a job. There won't be any wandering around footloose when you get out."

"Maybe I should stay on here as a civilian."

"As my assistant? Don't be ridiculous. Besides, I'm looking forward to getting someone who believes in God."

Feeney had served as altar boy at Rabb's Mass and had tried in vain to get back again the feelings he had had as a kid performing those functions. Of course, it was a lot harder being an altar boy back then; things were more complicated and you had to memorize Latin responses you didn't understand but that in their very unintelligibility had added to the mystery of the ceremony. Feeney recalled the younger version of himself, innocent, full of hope, good as gold. Well, too much had happened in the interval and he watched Rabb go through the rite in a brisk fifteen minutes and it meant nothing to Feeney at all. What did it mean to Rabb? As far as Feeney could tell, it was a function the priest performed without emotion. Not many inmates came to the daily Mass and only a few of them received communion. Even if he had been attracted to the faith, communion would have been a stumbling block for Feeney, since he would have had to believe that the thin discs of bread were completely different after Rabb said the words "This is my body" over them. From flour and water to the body and blood of Jesus Christ. Feeney remembered making his First Communion at the age of eight, when he had accepted that dogma as easily he had the multiplication table or the English language.

"You can't hold that against me," he had told the chaplain. "Faith is a gift."

"Sure it is. And you gave it back."

"Haven't you ever had any doubts?"

"Now, don't try to tell me you had some great intellectual crisis, Feeney. It was booze and women and general bad living that came between you and God Almighty, not some logical problem."

That was probably true enough. In any case, Feeney had no desire to argue the point, not when the day of his freedom drew ever nearer and he lay in bed in a cold sweat thinking of it. He considered faking a return to religion so that Rabb would be more sympathetic but he sensed he would have had difficulty deceiving the chaplain, even if he could have brought himself to try. In the end, Rabb had come through with a job anyway, janitor at St. Hilary's parish in Fox River.

"The pastor is an alcoholic. Reformed. One of the most brilliant men in my class at the seminary. Knows all kinds of languages. Might have been a bishop if it hadn't been for the bottle."

This had led Feeney to expect a tragic personage or a nagging ex-drinker of the usual sort, but Dowling was a surprise. For one thing, he left him alone, almost too much. Feeney would almost have preferred a little more anxiety at having an ex-con around, maybe even a campaign to bring him back to Jesus. Well, he got anxiety in spades from Mrs. Murkin. The only thing he didn't like was the fact that Dowling's cop friend Keegan was always hanging around. Dowling had introduced them and again Feeney had expected the usual homily about the straight and narrow, but Keegan, like Dowling, just took him for what he was, or seemed to be, and that was that. It was almost an insult.

Upstairs, the two priests were now walking around, their voices got fainter, and Feeney heard a door slam. He tipped forward, bringing the front legs of his chair to the floor, and stood up. He tiptoed up the stairs, opened the kitchen door, and was face to face with Marie Murkin. She let out a screech and threw up her hands, but then, seeing who it was, got angry as hell.

"What do you mean, creeping up on me like that?"

"I didn't know you were here."

"What are you doing down in the basement anyway? Father Dowling and Father Rabb just went over the school to find you."

Feeney nodded and went out the back door. Jesus H. Christ, what a woman. She had scared him as much as he had her. When he got to the street, he saw Rabb and Dowling going in the front door of the school. Suddenly he was truly scared. They would go to his room and, if he knew Rabb, walk in and snoop around. As an ex-con, he would have no right to privacy in Rabb's eyes. He had lived in a fishbowl for years, subject to a surprise shakedown any time the screws felt like it. These months at St. Hilary's had made him careless; he had actually come to think of that room as his, off-limits to everyone else. But he could not bring himself to lock the door. He had had to shag some of those old birds away who seemed to think they had the run of the whole school, including the caretaker's room, yet he had had no hesitation about hiding the gun he found in the snow in his room. What the hell he had wanted to keep it for he didn't know. It wasn't loaded. The fact was that he had all but forgotten it, after squirreling it away in a drawer beneath his socks and underwear.

Feeney took the long way around to the school, going over one block and coming back across the snow-covered playground and slipping in a back door. He went up to the second floor by the back staircase and then scooted down the hall to the stairway that descended to his room. He went halfway down and then sat on a step, waiting. He could feel his heart pound.

What the hell kind of a story could he come up with when Rabb found the pistol in his room? Truth was an unfamiliar terrain and he had little desire to start across it, particularly when he was certain any mention of those three men and two trucks would get him into a hell of a lot more trouble than he would be in with Rabb and Dowling over the gun.

Then he heard them below, and an old woman's voice too, and he fled up the stairs and loped down the upstairs corridor to the stairway up which he had come. As he went down it, the backs of his legs felt like jelly. In fact, he felt weak all over and it was easy to imagine himself just collapsing and rolling like a boneless ball to the bottom of the stairs. But he made it to the bottom all right, pulled open the door into the lower hall, and for the second time in fifteen minutes was face to face with a frightened woman. Jennie.

"Oh my," she said in a choked whisper. "You scared the piss out of me."

"I'm sorry."

"You ought to be." Then she regained her composure and the sly smile he did not like at all. "You've had visitors, Mr. Feeney. Some of your clerical friends."

"Is that right?"

"They seemed to think you've been hiding something. I wonder what it would have been."

"Did they take anything?"

She stepped back and assumed an air of theatrical surprise. "What on earth would they have found to take?"

Again she gave him that goddamn knowing smile and he thought how easy it would be to take that scrawny neck in his bare hands and squeeze the life out of her.

24

AT FOUR o'clock in the afternoon the light had already begun to fade and, as Cy Horvath drove along the river road in the direction of Liberati's marina, the distinction between the mottled snow and the air above it grew blurred while the surface of the river, rippling and frigid, was dull gray. Leafless trees stood out against this wintry background and might have suggested to a mind more poetic than Horvath's arthritic fingers clawing at the sky. His thoughts were quite prosaic. He was wondering how he might corroborate the things he had heard from Charmaine the previous day. Someone that willing to talk would find it equally easy to forget what she had said if he tried to use her as a witness. Nonetheless, her mindless remarks had permitted Horvath to construct a plausible drama to account for the deaths of Enoch Hingle and Stevie O'Brien.

The clothes in which Enoch Hingle had been found

dead had been retained by the lab, and another examination conducted with an eye to drugs had turned up some granules in the pocket of Hingle's jacket.

"Marijuana," Solomon said tonelessly when Horvath answered his summons. "Do you have a cigarette?"

"No."

"Good. I'm trying to quit." But all the while they spoke, Solomon's hand kept going to the breast pocket of his lab jacket and coming back empty. The Chicago police had found out where Hingle was living. The name he was using wasn't on any of the credit cards and ID found on the body. The landlady phoned in when he failed to come home and a little checking established that her missing roomer was Enoch Hingle. There was a supply of pills and marijuana in the room of sufficient quantity to suggest a dealer, rather than a user with a deep sense of insecurity about supply. So both dead men had been engaged in small-bore drug traffic. That was a plausible explanation in Hingle's case; in Stevie O'Brien's, it was simple fact. No matter how minor an operation theirs might have been, it would have been sufficient threat to the big boys, those who had control of the likes of Gruening, Albini and DiNigro. So the interlopers had been removed.

Captain Keegan had listened to all this with a disapproving frown on his face and Horvath suddenly wished he had a lot more evidence than he did.

"You're linking Hingle and Stevie?"

"Yes. But that really isn't necessary."

"No. I suppose you could ask Martin if he ever heard of Hingle under some name or other."

Horvath nodded. Keegan had not sounded exactly encouraging. If Horvath had not known of the captain of detectives' long friendship with Iggie O'Brien, he would have felt let down by his boss.

"The real question, Captain, is where does Liberati fit into all this."

"If he does."

So Horvath told Keegan about the conversation with Charmaine. Keegan was a good deal more receptive to this information. "Where the hell was Liberati when the two shootings occurred?"

"He isn't going to volunteer that information and I have no way to force it from him."

"That goddamn Tuttle."

However much of a pain in the neck Tuttle might be, he was not the problem. Drugs no longer elicited the kind of response they once had: indignant editorials, public demands that those trafficking in drugs be put away for life, prosecutors willing to embark on a crusade. People had simply become bored with the subject. In this Robertson was typical, rather than the reverse. Drugs? Ho hum. The fact that there were two dead bodies did not really change matters. The idea seemed to be that, if people like Hingle and Stevie O'Brien were violating the law, it was economical that they should have been handled by others of their kind. Of course no one would have endorsed this as a policy if it were so baldly stated. It was rather a matter of a tacit philosophy that seemed to lie behind the tendency to inaction and lack of burning interest. Horvath was almost sorry the drug angle had come up, since it obscured the brutal reality of the riddled body of Enoch Hingle and the wet frozen corpse that had been Stevie O'Brien.

Liberati. It didn't take a genius to see he could hardly be an innocent party. Too many things connected him with what had happened: the truck, the fact that he was a client of Owlize, the weapon used. Horvath would have liked to take possession of every .22 pistol Liberati owned. Not that he really thought the murder weapon would be found among them.

"Or weapons," Keegan growled.

"No. Weapon. Solomon is sure they were both killed with the same gun."

"So that is the link?"

"That's the link."

"Yeah. But a missing link. All we have to do is find it."

Well, not quite all. If they found it, they would have to prove who used it. Even if it turned out to be one of Liberati's pistols, he could deny knowledge of how it had gotten into the hands of a killer. Stolen? He could even claim a pattern of not reporting stolen items. In any case, suspicion would turn to one or all of his salesmen and it could happen that a conviction would be had easily. To pin a crime on someone already guilty of others was a comparatively simple thing to do. So that is how it might go. If they had the .22.

Horvath's notion that Liberati had to be involved was not due simply to the fact that he did not like the man, though he didn't like him. There was something distasteful about a man that age still unmarried, still catting around with a string of women. Was Charmaine one of them? There had always been such women in Liberati's life.

Of course Liberati's life came down largely to what Horvath could glean from the meager police record that admittedly stopped some years back. But every other time Liberati had figured in a police report, it had been because of a woman. The other times were due to commotions at the marina. The fact that some at least of those commotions were related to drug usage pricked Horvath's curiosity as, years before, it had Iggie O'Brien's: A place like Liberati's marina was almost inevitably going to be connected with smoking pot, and that said nothing either way about Liberati's involvement in it. If it had, it would have implicated Liberati's father, Carlo.

The son still lived with the widowed father, which, despite himself, gained Horvath's grudging approval. You would have expected a libertine like the son to have a bachelor pad, but he remained in his father's house and more or less looked after the old man. During the day, Carlo Liberati was at St. Hilary's parish center, but aside from that he was at home. Horvath heard he still helped out at the marina, even though management of the place had passed to his son. Winter was the problem, evidently, and Horvath supposed that was the reason old Carlo went off most days to St. Hilary's.

When he approached the marina, he began to slow down, but then he applied his foot to the gas again and continued at an even speed. There was a car parked in the parking lot. Tracks from the road led to it standing solitary in the snow-filled lot. Whoever had driven in like that was running a risk of getting stuck, and it would be no easy thing to get help out on that stretch of river road, all but deserted at this time of year. Horvath went on by and could see no sign of an occupant of the parked car. And then he caught a glimpse of a figure out on the dock and Horvath slowed and stopped. He backed up slowly and came to a halt just short of the entrance to the marina.

The parked car must have had to gun it to get through the bank of snow created by the plow blocking the entrance. Another risky move. It would have been easy for the car to get hung up on that icy ridge. Horvath got out of his car and eased the door shut, then stood for a moment listening to the silence. God, how quiet it was. There was a slight mournful sound of the wind scudding across the crisp surface of the snow, rattling the bare branches of the trees. In summer there would have been the happy shouts of bathers and on the river there would have been sunfish sailboats rented from the marina, and some canoes too. Now the river seemed sluggish, too cold to make any sound. When he started to walk, Horvath's shoes made a squeaky, eerie sound on the frozen snow.

He walked in the tire tracks the car had made but, when they turned off into the lot, he had to go through quite deep snow. It was higher than his shoe tops and when it got deeper still he could feel it on his bare legs above his socks. He lifted his knees high and put out his arms to retain his balance, all the while trying to be as quiet as he could. He could not see the dock now, his vision of it blocked by the main building. Board awnings had been let down over the screen windows and locked against the winter and, to his right, the boathouse and johns and bathhouse were similarly battened down. All the buildings were of frame construction and the paint, white with red trim, looked almost bright despite the waning light.

A boardwalk encircled the main building but it was buried beneath the snow. The railing was of some help now, and Horvath paused to study the footprints made by the person who was out there on the dock. He was surprised to see they were a woman's. Had it been a woman he saw on the dock? Maybe it was a man wearing cowboy boots.

At the corner of the building, a sloping pile of ice had formed from water dripping from the roof caused by snow thawed in the sun. It was on this ice that Horvath lost his footing. He reached out for the railing with his flailing hand and, when he grasped it, there was the sharp crack of wood giving way beneath his full weight. From the corner the dock was visible and, as he regained his footing, Horvath looked to see a woman on the dock turn and stare at him with wide, frightened eyes as her mouth opened in a scream.

25

NOSTALGIA was one thing curled on a couch at night with a bourbon and 7-up and Frankie's golden oldies on the machine. What harm did it do then to dream of what used to be and of what might have been, indulging in self-pity? Life was hard, even when it was easy. Sometimes the happy times were the saddest of all because you knew they couldn't last. Everything slipped away into the darkness and there was nothing to do to stop it. You might slow it down with a transplant, a face lift, or by getting married again and pretending you were at the beginning of life. And you could sing songs about doing it your way, defiant, brave, but kind of silly too. But Evelyn loved it. Frank Sinatra was someone she could understand, relate to, and she was sure he would understand her too, really understand her.

The odd identification of Sinatra and Robbie Liberati intensified after Jennie mentioned his old man. Evelyn's memory of Carlo Liberati was vivid and he was not an old man in her memories. His hair had turned gray early, as Robbie's had too, and there were deep lines from his nose to the corners of his mouth. He had what she had thought of as a year-long sun tan. The Liberatis dodged the sun and were brown as berries while their customers laid themselves out on the sand to broil and left groaning with sunburn. Evelyn had tanned easily, but it always took her a long time to achieve the shade she wanted. Back then, in the days of one-piece suits and generally undaring beach attire, Evelyn had been a bit of a pacesetter on the beach of the Liberati marina. When she lay on her stomach she would untie the strings of her halter in order to get an even tan across her back, and it had been an added pleasure, lying there, feeling the attention she was getting. Old Mr. Liberati had noticed too.

The first time Evelyn looked up directly into the steady gaze of Carlo Liberati she had felt an impulse to tie her halter strings and throw a towel over her shoulders. That was when she still thought something might come of her and Robbie and she did not want to make a bad impression on his parents. But even that first time she was aware of Mr. Liberati seated in the shade next to the marina main building with the long sleeves of his shirt buttoned at the wrists, a felt hat on top of head, a shadowy figure in the shade of the wooden awning, she sensed that he was looking at her in exactly the same way his son did. He was looking at her the way a man looks at a woman.

Of course he had seemed impossibly old to her and she could not really believe he was still interested in women. In girls. She still thought of herself as a girl. But she had changed her mind about Mr. Liberati as the days passed. It had become a little unspoken arrangement between them: she would lay out her towel—that her favorite spot was always free was not, it turned out, an accident—lie down and, after a minute or two, undo her halter. When she looked at him over the tops of her sunglasses, his eyes would be on her. Sometimes, as if thoughtlessly, she would lift up from the blanket, giving him a real look as she pretended to be distracted by some activity on the beach. It was shameless teasing, but she thought it was harmless. Helping an old man remember, that is how she had thought of it. And she enjoyed it. It was one of those occasions when she had learned something about herself that should have shocked her and didn't. It turned out it was not all that harmless.

While Robbie was around, old Carlo did nothing but look, but when the son was absent he became bolder. He sent a beer to Evelyn and tipped his hat when she acknowledged it. She sat up, pressing her still loosened halter to her in a maidenly way, and smiled at him as if in confusion. The beer was welcome and she would have liked to chug-a-lug it, but she sipped a little and put it down, making a little hollow for the bottle in the sand. Reaching behind her back to tie the halter strings, she sucked in her tummy and threw back her shoulders. More thanks for the beer.

And then there was the episode in the boathouse. He came up behind her without warning and put his arms around her before she knew what was going on. She did not turn around. The long white sleeves and mild garlicky breath told her who it was. She said nothing and neither did he. They stood there, he pressing against her, and the dank smell from the soaked wood of the boathouse, the sun on the spangled surface of the river, the oddly echoing voices of the bathers and boaters, etched themselves in her memory. That was when she realized she had no chance at all with Robbie. Both father and son saw her simply as a target of opportunity. This angered her, and she broke away from the old man and sprinted across the hot sand to where she had left her towel. She picked it up, slung her beach bag over her shoulder, and marched out to her car.

And sat in it. Waiting. He came. He stood at the driver's side, put his hand on the roof of the car, and looked toward the beach, surveying it with eyes shaded by the brim of his hat.

"Look, I meant no harm. I scared you. I'm sorry."

"You didn't scare me. You surprised me."

He looked down at her and his eyes crinkled nicely. "You are a beautiful woman."

"I date your son. You know that."

He shrugged. He reached in and put his hand on her bare shoulder. She did not stop him when he slid his hand down her back, but when he reached the tie string of her halter she moved away from him.

"Don't."

That was that. She drove away and had forgotten the incident before she was halfway back to town. That night she went out with Robbie, and when they left the bar and were walking to his car and he tugged her to him, he suggested they go to her place.

"Let's go to yours, Robbie. We never go there."

"Evelyn, my parents are home. What could we do?"

"You could introduce me to them."

He did not quite stop in time a little noise of incredulity. "You know my father already and my mother—look, do you know anything about Italian mothers?"

"What do you mean, I know your father?"

"You see him at the marina."

"I've seen your mother there too."

"Okay. That's what I mean. You know them, so what's the point?"

"They don't know me."

He stopped and looked at her, his arms extended, hands open, head cocked to one side. It was half a minute before he shrugged, took her arm, and led her to the car. "Okay. You want to meet my parents, you'll meet my parents."

Not quite. The Liberati house was built on the bluff above the marina and the access road was private, a long driveway rather than a road. The house had begun as a modest cottage and had grown from that, architecturally overdone and some parts in conflict with other parts, but it was a monument to Carlo Liberati's affluence and the fact that he had succeeded in America. Besides, the taxes were low out there. He had none of the disadvantages of city life and the advantages of city life came to him, to his marina. The house was set serenely above the sometimes frantic activity of the marina, and if both Carlo and his wife spent most of each summer day and half the night at the marina, they could withdraw to the seclusion of their house on the bluff and be sovereigns of a good deal of what they surveyed below.

That night, when he approached the house, Robbie slowed down and proceeded at a crawl up the driveway.

"What's wrong?"

"Maybe this isn't a good night to meet the folks, Evelyn."

"How do you know?"

They had come into a parking area and Robbie proceeded to make a U-turn. They were three huge Cadillacs already parked there and, as they turned to go away, Evelyn was aware of a man behind the wheel of one of the cars. He might have been a boxer, both in the athletic and canine senses of the term. His small eyes took her in and she had the fleeting impression of someone cruel and without feeling.

"That man looks like a gangster," she said to Robbie.

"What the hell do you mean?"

"The man in the car—"

"Just forget the man in the car, okay? You didn't see

him. Jesus, why did you have to talk me into bringing you up here for anyway?"

He was like a little kid who has done something dumb and expects to be punished for it. Maybe it was his reaction more than the expression on the driver's face that imprinted the occasion in her memory. She came to think of the Liberati house as a mysterious place. Menacing, but in an attractive way, a little like Gatsby's house.

"Who the hell's Gatsby?" Robbie demanded. He had entered his violently jealous phase.

"Just a friend, Robbie. He's dead now."

"Oh. I'm sorry."

Freighted with memories of the father and son, full of the bittersweet realization that the past was gone forever yet capable of being evoked by an old song, a place, Evelyn had driven out to the Liberati marina and it seemed right, in a crazy sort of way, that it should be winter when she went back. The closed-up buildings, the drifts of snow, the sluggish bitterly cold look of the river, matched her sense that this place was an item in the irrecoverable past, no part of the present.

She bumped into the driveway off the river road, negotiating the bank of snow thrown up by the county plow, and turned into the parking lot, snow crunching beneath the tires of the car. It was deeper than she had expected. Maybe it would be smart to just back out again, trying to use the tracks she had just made. But first she wanted to sit here and remember. She lit a cigarette. There had been cigarettes of another sort available here years ago, joints, and everyone assumed that old Liberati was in on their sale. No one cared. It was no more important than underage kids buying beer at the marina. Everyone knew Italians drank as soon as they were weaned. It didn't mean anything. Evelyn had tried pot, but she only enjoyed it with Robbie. It was an aphrodisiac as far as she was concerned, slowing him down, making it better.

After a time she got out of the car and walked around to the river side of the building. The dock, unlike the boardwalk, was clear of snow, perhaps swept clean by the wind, and Evelyn walked out to the end of the dock as much to get out of the snow as to elicit more thoughts of long ago. As she stood there, her eyes smarted in the wind and the tears came and she welcomed them. Oh, dear God, how sweetly sad it was to stand here and recall those days that once had been. She squeezed her eyes shut and tears beaded on her cheeks. Would they freeze? The possibility seemed romantic. Donne. A bracelet of bright hair about the bone. Why did she remember things like that? She did not read much, but she had her little inventory of literary memories, more precious for being few. Emily Dickinson was her favorite poet.

There was a sharp sound behind her and she wheeled to see a man in an odd posture at the corner of the marina building, and before she realized what she was doing, she screamed. The next minute was timeless. Steady now, the man advanced to the dock. He stopped and they stood facing each other. It was a Brontë scene. Or out of a Western movie. She could not make out the man's face, but he was huge. The image of the driver of the Cadillac from years ago came to her. She seemed not to have drawn a breath since she stopped screaming. And then the man called to her.

"I'm Lieutenant Horvath, ma'am. From the Fox River police."

"Don't come near me!"

But he did. He had taken something from his pocket and was holding it out to her, and when she saw the badge she almost fainted with relief. She actually ran to him and he put his arms around her. Heathcliff. Heathcliff. She was sobbing against the rough nap of of his coat.

He took her arm and led her back to the marina building. "Watch this ice," he said when they rounded the corner of the building. "I nearly broke my neck on it."

"You did break the railing." Her voice trembled. Why in the name of God was she so frightened? Her tears were almost hysterical now, the tears of relief. For an awful moment on the end of the dock she had felt more vulnerable than she ever had before in her life, with the icy river behind and the huge figure of a man blocking her way to the shore.

He got into her car with her and told her to start the motor and turn on the heater, which she did. It was good to follow orders and do what she was told. Why the hell had she made this stupid pilgrimage to Liberati's marina?

Lieutenant Horvath was easy to talk to. Within minutes she found herself telling him what this place had been like in summer years ago.

"I know. I used to come here as a kid."

She looked at him. When he was a kid and when she was a kid were not times that had coincided.

"It was run by a family named Liberati."

"It still is," he said. "By the son. Did you know him?"

She smiled enigmatically. "Oh, yes. I knew him."

And then she was babbling away about those sunny summer days, the humid nights, dates with Robbie. She might have gone on to tell Lieutenant Horvath about old Carlo too, he was that easy to talk to, but it was getting quite dark now.

"Why don't you see if you can get out of here all right?"

"Aren't you going to arrest me?"

"What for?"

"I don't know. Trespassing?"

"Not this time."

She had already told him who she was and where she lived, half wondering if the interest he showed might lead to something else, but then she noticed the wedding band on his huge finger and she was certain he was the kind of man who would not deny by his actions the significance of that ring. And she liked that. She needed to believe there were people in the world who kept their promises, were faithful, lived by the rules. Unless she was an exception, the world would be a hell of a place to live in.

She started to back up and the wheels began to spin, so she let him take over and he managed to get the car on the river road, gunning it through the snowdrift that blocked the entrance of the driveway.

"I'm sorry I frightened you," he said before getting out of the car.

"Better you than someone else."

He looked at her, holding the door open. "You mean better me than Liberati?"

She answered with her enigmatic smile. It was an instinct with her, trying to make him see her as a woman, but again she knew it was hopeless. She watched him walk swiftly to the car parked farther up the road, then turned the wheel and started back to Fox River.

26

MARCUS RIEHLE had never had writer's block during the two decades he had been perfecting his talents and then living by his pen. Now for the first time he sat at his typewriter and stared at the keyboard and the arrangement of letters seemed something he had never seen before. He put the tips of his fingers on the keys. A S D F for the left hand, J K L for the right. He exerted a slight pressure. Nothing happened. He had not yet turned on the machine. Its hum, given his inability to write, had the disturbing accusative sound of a taxi meter. The sheet of paper he had rolled into the machine was a virgin expanse of white. Martha Ennis.

Marcus brought his hands to his face and huddled over the typewriter as if in physical pain. Oh, the humiliation. The whole world knew of his stupid adolescent infatuation for Mrs. Ennis; what was worse, everyone knew of his writings as well.

When Father Dowling stopped by to see him, Marcus Riehle had been on the alert for amusement or condescension in the priest's manner. He detected none. Well, Dowling was a priest, a good man; his reaction could hardly be taken as typical.

"I feel bad that I never connected you with the name on all those pamphlets. Imagine, a member of the parish writing those."

"Am I a member of the parish?"

"You attend Mass at Saint Hilary's, don't you?"

"I'm not a contributor. I mean, I don't have envelopes. I do put money in the collection plate."

Father Dowling dismissed this with a wave of his hand. It occurred to Marcus Riehle that he was having no difficulty speaking with the priest.

"I see you now give away pamphlets free, Father." No stammer, no hesitation; he spoke without impediment. Was it possible that now, when he had reached the nadir of obloquy, he was free of the thorn in his flesh, his tongue loosed? Maybe that was why he was unable to write.

"I saw you at Enoch Hingle's wake, Marcus."

"And burial!"

"That was very thoughtful of you."

"They arrested me."

"That was a dreadful mistake. Captain Keegan feels very bad about it. He will tell you that himself. But you can imagine how frantic the police are with two murders and no solution."

"Did they really think I had something to do with those murders?" He could not get indignation into his voice, marveling at the easy flow of words emerging trippingly on the tongue that had always blocked them before. Would thinking of stuttering bring it back? Apparently not.

"It is their job to be suspicious. Mooney the undertaker

was struck by your presence at the wake. Strange man. Why would he assume that mourning is not genuine?"

"I wasn't mourning Enoch Hingle. I was thinking of writing a novel about him."

Roger Dowling, far from being shocked, leaned forward with new interest. "Then you must have thought of an explanation of his murder."

Marcus looked thoughtful. "It would be unwise for me to adhere too closely to the facts of his life. Artistically unwise."

"I understand. But the artistic imagination might be able to see something the police are overlooking. How much do you know of the circumstances of Hingle's death?"

Marcus was surprised at how informed Father Dowling was on the matter. The priest's voice was precise, yet somehow sad, as he re-created for Marcus the drama of the truck towed to the street next to the rectory and abandoned there with the lifeless body of Enoch Hingle in the cab. Marcus became fascinated with the narrative, with the indication that Hingle had been involved in drugs. A gangland killing? But it was the recurrence of the name Liberati that set what Father Dowling had called his artistic imagination going.

"You know the Liberatis?" Roger Dowling asked.

"Know them? I know of them. They have a beach on the river where we used to go when we were kids."

How matter-of-fact a remark, yet what heartbreak it concealed. And the phony "we," as if Marcus Riehle, foot-loose happy boy, surrounded by friends, had whiled away delightful hours at the marina. The truth was a sadder thing. Roly-poly Marcus, ignored when not actively shunned by others his age, his delicate skin blistering with sunburn rather than browning to the desired tan, sipping cream soda in the shadow of the building, surveying with inarticulate longing the half acre of human flesh basting in its own juices. His single success, if it could be called that, was Evelyn. She had let him buy her an ice cream bar. With her own money. He was at the head of the line, she did not want to wait ten or fifteen minutes to reach the counter, she asked him to buy her ice cream for her.

He did. It might have been a betrothal, though it was an all but wordless bargain. He had trusted himself to do no more than smile in response to her thanks, a diffident toss of his head. He watched her walk away across the sand, and suddenly the beach seemed a symbol of the sacrifices lovers make for each other.

From that afternoon, his going to the marina had the note of keeping a rendezvous. The relationship between himself and Evelyn remained wordless. An observer might not have detected any relationship at all between them. But in the imagination of Marcus Riehle the remainder of the summer was defined by the fated, romantic, mute passion shared by Evelyn and himself.

It was some years later, after he had been in the service, the summer before the experience in Peoria that turned him into a writer, that Evelyn betrayed him. She had been married and divorced, he knew that. The first time he saw her spread her towel upon the beach and arrange her even more womanly figure upon it, he saw her as a tragic figure, a wounded bird, someone he might comfort and make whole again. Perhaps her marriage had not been valid and the divorce presented no impediment. But the impediment that mattered was that in his speech. No matter how often he rehearsed the scene he thought of as reunion, it fell apart when, having swaggered across the sand with an ice cream bar, he stopped where she lay and offered it to her. And was unable to speak. But then a metaphorical shadow came between the sun of innocence and Evelyn on the beach. The Liberatis. Both of them.

Marcus tried to see the bizarre situation in terms of

some impossibly complicated Greek tragedy, but somehow it always came through as Restoration farce. Father and son in pursuit of the same woman and she the willing target of both. At first Marcus treated the inescapable facts as a terrible temptation he must repulse. It was unworthy of him to think that Evelyn could possibly . . . But it was common knowledge that she dated Rob Liberati and when Marcus saw the father, Carlo, embracing Evelyn in the boathouse and could detect not the slightest sign of resistance in his beloved, he turned sadly and definitively away. It was a relief to go back to Peoria in September.

When he began to write he had tried with several kinds of unsuccess to reduce to fiction that strange trio at the marina. The version he had aimed at pulp magazines was probably the truest, no matter its artistic limitations. The novella featured two gangsters operating behind a façade of respectability, into the web of whose intrigues the fragile fly of an unsuspecting divorcée had been drawn. The story had climaxed in an orgy of violence, bodies were strewn upon the beach, the motorboat in which the Liberatis tried to escape across the river exploded in a geyser of poetic justice as the girl shuddered in the arms of the protagonist. So much for the drug traffic in the sleepy river town in the Midwest. It was an odd thought that his old flight of imagination might have been enacted in the death of Enoch Hingle.

"How does the death of the O'Brien boy fit into the picture?" Marcus asked Father Dowling.

The priest's expression altered slightly. "Tell me about your writing."

Marcus began diffidently enough, meaning to put himself down—what was he but a pamphleteer?—but it did not come out that way. His tongue seemed to have a mind of its own and the confidence with which he sketched his career lent it a nobility he had never before recognized in it. A long slide downhill from the heady aspirations of his beginnings to an undeniably prodigious production of pamphlets.

"You have done an immense amount of good," Father Dowling said. "I have read several of your recent things. Your pamphlet on how to change one's life seems to me full of sound advice. I suppose it reflects your personal philosophy."

Marcus admitted that it did. He went on, speaking as one having authority, and it was gratifying to have Father Dowling for an audience.

"I have passed it on to my housekeeper to read."

"Mrs. Murkin? Perhaps she will find in it further reason to accuse me."

"She too is contrite, Mr. Riehle."

"And Mrs. Ennis?"

"It's odd that you should ask. It's partly because of her that I have come calling on you. She is the leader of a local writers club that meets fortnightly at the public library."

"Is she?"

"She would very much like you to address her group."

"I can't imagine what I would have to say to them."

"You aren't serious. A writer of your experience? I should think you could give hopeful writers all kinds of pointers of a practical kind. Tell me more about your novel."

"It isn't wise to talk out a story before it is written. You run the risk of losing it."

"There, you see. That is the kind of advice you can give to others."

"Don't tell me you have ambitions to write, Father Dowling."

"Hardly. I have difficulty writing letters. I would much rather read." He looked around Marcus Riehle's apartment. Was he surprised to see so few books here? But a real writer has no time to read. "Can I tell Mrs. Ennis you will speak to her group?"

Vindication, when it comes, is anticlimactic. He imagined himself at the podium, looking out at the little band of hopefuls who gathered around Mrs. Ennis at the public library. Local author addresses writers club. He imagined Mrs. Ennis listening with rapt attention. So what? Did he really care what her opinion of him was? But he agreed to speak to the writers club.

Impending triumph, the apparent overcoming of his stammer, but the loss of his muse as well. Marcus Riehle, huddled over his typewriter, wept for the loss of the days of rejection, his inability to speak, the anonymity with which he had produced a mountain of pamphlets, one after another, flooding the churches of the nation. Would he ever be able to do that again? He thought of his projected novel and his body actually shook with fear. He could not do it. Was that his future: renown, oral fluency, literary impotence? And Mrs. Ennis?

After several minutes his head lifted, tears dried, and his vision cleared. A new significance of Father Dowling's visit formed itself slowly in his mind. Was he destined to perform now, not in the realm of imagination, but in real time and space? Had the pastor of St. Hilary's unwittingly set their ancient nemesis against the Liberatis? Marcus Riehle sat back and closed his eyes. A thoughtful expression occupied his face. He wondered how Evelyn, thrice-broken bird, would react to him now that he had been granted the gift of tongues.

27

WHEN EVELYN CUNNINGHAM telephoned Lieutenant Horvath, Cy found it difficult to believe her excuse for making the call.

"I don't want you to think I have a habit of wandering around other people's property, Lieutenant. Not that you weren't perfectly understanding at the time. But I suppose you have been wondering what I was doing out there at the marina."

"Or vice versa."

"What do you mean."

"That isn't exactly the regular beat of a Fox River detective."

"Ah hah. I never thought of that. What were you doing there?"

"Just making a routine check."

"On me?"

Her teasing intonation was one that the monogamous Horvath had come to recognize over the years, and familiarity with it had not diminished his contempt. People had a way of confiding in him and with some women confidence could be a prelude to something else. But a woman who made a play for a cop often had an ulterior purpose. What anxieties had been stirred up in Evelyn Cunningham by his surprising her at the Liberati marina? He had of course wondered what besides nostalgia had taken her out there on a bleak winter afternoon. The fact that her old flame Rob Liberati had figured in reports of the deaths of Enoch Hingle and the son of Iggie O'Brien seemed sufficient trigger for her sentimental journey back to the beach on the Fox River. Now her telephone call suggested that might be too simple an explanation. He asked Evelyn if she had a confession to make.

"If I did, I would find it easy to make it to you."

The invitation was unmistakable now. "I'll remember that."

"A funny thing. I came upon your picture in an old yearbook. I should have known you were an athlete."

"That was a long time ago."

She sighed along the wire. "Isn't it unbelievable how swiftly time passes?"

Cy Horvath was not inclined to philosophical reflection and was not tempted by Evelyn's suggestion they had memories in common that it would be amusing to dredge up together. He stopped the conversation by telling her he was wanted on another line.

"Oh, I'm so sorry. You must be very busy with all these murders."

He did not like the implication that the deaths of Hingle and Stevie O'Brien amounted to little more than an inconvenience for himself. After he had hung up he sat for a moment staring impassively at the telephone. At first he thought of Evelyn Cunningham, but his thoughts soon returned to the investigation. When he heaved to his feet and started for Keegan's office his mind was made up.

"Robertson would hit the roof," Keegan said, when Cy had told his captain what they might do.

"We can do it without checking with him. Get a warrant and confiscate all Liberati's .22s and let Robertson do whatever he wants to do after the fact."

"Cy, do you really think we'll find the weapon?"

"If we don't do this we're as bad as Robertson."

Keegan took that hard and Cy didn't blame him, but it was the truth. They knew that the same weapon had killed Hingle and Stevie O'Brien. They were morally certain that Rob Liberati's salesmen were involved in the dispatching of Enoch. This was the connection they needed; Liberati was the middle term that linked Enoch Hingle and Stevie O'Brien. The weapon was taken back to the used-car lot after Hingle was killed and it didn't matter that those three salesmen were in custody when Stevie was killed. They had been Liberati's agents in the killing of Enoch Hingle and Liberati himself was free on the night of Stevie's murder.

"And Liberati killed him?"

"Or someone did it for him."

"Someone."

"Captain, Liberati is the man we're after."

Keegan turned his chair and looked out the window. "You may be right. But there is the little matter of evidence. Finding the weapon would help one hell of a lot, but we wouldn't find it in Liberati's collection."

"Someone dumb enough to murder is dumb enough to keep the weapon."

"Liberati isn't dumb. He has reported a theft." Keegan

turned and looked at Horvath. "One of his .22 pistols is missing."

Keegan seemed to expect some alteration in Horvath's expression but Horvath knew his face looked the same rain or shine. But he was startled by this.

"How did he identify the missing pistol?"

"In two ways. He had its serial number, but there is an easier way to identify it. It has his father's name engraved on the barrel."

"It's his father's gun?"

"It was. He gave it to the son."

"And now it's missing."

Horvath felt that Keegan should have told him this right away when he suggested getting a warrant and confiscating Liberati's collection of .22 pistols.

"Missing and probably unfindable."

Horvath thought of the lake on whose frozen surface the body of Stevie O'Brien had been found. Whatever clues might have been found in the snow and ice around the fishing shack had been obliterated by thaw and Howard Charles's tramping around. If the gun that had killed both Enoch and Stevie were on the bottom of that lake there was little chance of their finding it. But of course it could be anywhere.

"I'm sorry, Cy."

Sorry was not the word for what Horvath felt. This was the damndest situation he had ever heard of. After his conversation with Charmaine, after the knowledge that the same weapon had been used in both murders, after the arrest of the Liberati sales force, Horvath was certain Liberati was the man they sought. Keegan knew it too. Without the weapon, they had evidence, but it was easy to imagine what could be done with it in court. Even the abandoned truck with Hingle's body in it could become lost in a barrage of lawyer talk. Would having the .22 really change that?

Agnes Lamb was waiting for him in his office. She got up when he entered and did not sit down again until he had. Horvath wasn't sure what he thought about Agnes's sense of protocol. But it was clear she wasn't being ironic in her exaggerated deference to superiors. Maybe the explanation was the one she offered. She meant to be the best cop she could possibly be.

"She wasn't lying," Agnes said. "She and Carlo Liberati are friends."

"For what that's worth."

"That's not all. She's friends with the son too."

Horvath looked at her. Her hair was pulled tightly back on her head and this accented her high round cheekbones. Agnes had a way of lifting her chin after speaking, punctuating what she had said.

"Friends," Horvath said.

Agnes brought out her notebook from the purse slung over her shoulder. "Here are the gory details."

Agnes's informant, the superintendent of Charmaine's building, was black, and that might have explained why he had been so forthcoming with her. She had been wearing civvies when she talked with him. The man, Leroy, knew both the Liberatis as visitors to Charmaine's apartment. Did the father know about the son or vice versa? Leroy doubted it. Horvath somehow found it easy that Charmaine should pursue so risky a line. From talking to her himself, he would have put her on Carlo's side, rather than Robbie's. No doubt that is what she had wanted him to think. Agnes saved the crusher for the end.

"Robbie was at her apartment the night young O'Brien was killed."

"He's sure of it?"

She nodded.

"That's interesting."

"Just interesting?"

"That isn't what Robbie told us. He said he was with his father that night."

"Just being discreet, I suppose."

There was no mistaking the irony in Agnes's voice. He told her about the report of the missing .22. Her brows rose.

"That's interesting too," she said.

Horvath looked across at Agnes. She was good, as good as he had thought she would be. She sat there now, waiting to be told what to do next.

"Agnes, find out all you can about Charmaine."

She rose immediately. "Should I work with Pianone?"

"No."

In the moment of hesitation, she seemed to be about to say something that would have altered his opinion of her. Horvath was relieved when, saying nothing more, she left the office.

28

CARLO LIBERATI was in his own eyes a public benefactor. No one knew the efforts he had made to prevent Fox River from being turned into another Cicero or Calumet City. But he had made those efforts and he had succeeded. The marina could never have survived as the more or less honest operation it was if things had gotten out of hand and the others had moved in, so he kept things at a level sufficient to persuade the more ambitious in Chicago that Fox River should be left alone. Fox River belonged to Carlo Liberati.

He had acquired the ability not to imagine the consequences of the modest operations he engaged in, using the marina as a shield. With drugs that was easy. He could look out over his beach filled with happy people and, if he thought of it at all, tell himself that he was responsible for their happiness.

Drugs were like booze, a neutral item; it was not his problem if some people abused them. He had resisted having a string of girls, but that too he had done, sporadically, to prevent others from moving in and making it worse. When the pressure dropped, he shagged the girls out of town. Juke boxes he had turned into an all but legitimate enterprise and had set a tone that was later adopted by others. If he used pirated records, that was simply good business, something any enterprising operator would have done if he had had the opportunity. Carlo had had the opportunity because of his origins. His origins were both a help and a danger. That was what Roberto could not seem to understand.

Roberto did not understand that they had control of Fox River only so long as they kept the others out. It was because of Roberto that those three hoods had muscled into the used-car lot and showed Roberto what had to be done when punks began poaching on the Fox River operation.

"He didn't even know about Hingle," Charmaine told Carlo.

"Now he knows."

"I'm not sure he believes it yet. He wants to go straight."

Charmaine smiled. Carlo did not. He was ashamed of his feelings for the girl. Anna had never given him any occasion to feel jealousy, so the emotion had been a new one for Carlo Liberati. Charmaine was playing several sides of the street and Carlo knew it, but he could not bring himself simply to drop her. He had never dropped a girl under such circumstances and he was too old to learn now.

Too old. He did not feel old when he whiled away the daytime hours at St. Hilary's Recreation Center. Jennie Carr helped. It was boring, but life was boring. For most of his life Carlo had made friends with boredom. The marina had been boring. Boredom was another name for peace. If he had wanted excitement, he wouldn't have bothered keeping others from moving into Fox River. He had not liked it when the truck containing Enoch Hingle's body had been left on the street beside the rectory. That had been meant as a warning to him as well as to Robbie. But what had really shaken him was when Jennie showed him the pistol.

"Where the hell did you get that?"

"Is it real?"

"Let me see."

She held it back, wanting to play a game, but Carlo took it from her with one swift motion and put it in his pocket. He told her it was real.

"You didn't even look at it."

"Tell me where you got it."

She was as crazy as she seemed. Carlo had noticed Feeney around, an odd sort of guy, looking into the gym furtively, then quickly disappearing. Once in a while he had seen Feeney shoveling the walks. He looked like a type Carlo had seen often in his life. What was a guy like that doing working at a church? Well, what was he himself doing spending his days in the parish center playing games with Jennie Carr? She had found the gun in Feeney's room. Carlo wondered about that. Was Feeney part of it?

"How did you get into his room?" he asked Jennie.

"It wasn't locked."

"He'll know it was you."

"How could he?"

"You're the only one crazy enough to go snooping around other people's rooms."

Jennie took it as a compliment. Carlo set up the checkerboard. It was a way to shut up Jennie, playing checkers, and he wanted to think.

"I hate living with my daughter," Jennie said. It was a familiar lament.

"You should be glad. You might be alone."

"You're alone."

He had told her of Roberto, as little as he could while retaining her companionship. Jennie was seventy-seven, five years older than he. Carlo thought of her as belonging to another generation. He had thought of Anna the same way, although she had been only a year older. Whenever Jennie got onto this loneliness business or complained about living with her daughter Evelyn, Carlo knew what she was after, but he played dumb. The thought was not even funny. Did she think he would replace Charmaine with herself? Not that Jennie knew of Charmaine. Carlo made sure Jennie was on her way home before he went to the car where Charmaine waited for him. That was how, after all these years, he had seen Evelyn again.

Evelyn. If he did replace Charmaine, he wouldn't mind going back to Evelyn. But he couldn't drop Charmaine, not when she was doublecrossing him. Roberto was all right, that was part of her job, keeping tabs on his son. Her job. Sometimes he wondered if Charmaine did work for him.

Roberto refused to talk with him about the arrest of his three salesmen.

"It's a message, Roberto."

"And one they'll pay for sending. I should never have taken them on."

"You had no choice."

"Don't tell me I've got no choice. You had a choice. If you'd made the right choice a long time ago, they wouldn't be bothering me at all."

It hurt to be treated that way by his own son. Roberto should appreciate what he had done. Roberto was a rich man and didn't even know it. At least he would be. Carlo could not quite grasp the fact of his own mortality, but he had provided well for Roberto. The boy should guess that and show more gratitude.

"He's scared," Charmaine said.

"Good."

A little fear was good. Charmaine could use some herself. When she got it, she had wept in his arms and Carlo had consoled her, patting her heaving shoulders, running his hand through her blonde hair while he thought to himself, "You cheating bitch, you cheating bitch."

When he gave the .22 back to Jennie he told her to put it in Feeney's room, right where she had found it. She looked at the pistol as if she had forgotten it.

"He shouldn't have a gun!"

"No one should. But he's the caretaker here."

"Some caretaker."

But she took it. He made sure she put it in the janitor's room, watching from the end of the hall. Afterward, she came back to him with a little expectant smile.

"Good girl," Carlo said.

29

ROGER DOWLING found the pistol lying on his desk at one o'clock in the afternoon. He had just come in from the church, where he had been reading his breviary and, when he saw the pistol, his eye drawn irresistibly to it as soon as he entered the room, he stopped and stared at it, then wheeled and hurried into the kitchen. Mrs. Murkin was not there. He heard her footsteps above. She was in her room. This was the hour of her siesta. He went back to the study.

The gun had not been on his desk twenty minutes before. After saying the noon Mass, he had had a sandwich and a glass of milk—a Lenten collation, in the old phrase—standing in the kitchen despite Marie Murkin's protest that this was insufficient nourishment, and then had gone into the study to fetch his breviary. It had been on his desk. He would certainly have noticed the pistol if it had been there then.

He took a pencil and tried to insert it into the barrel of the pistol but it would not fit. The narrow blade of his pipe knife did. He picked up the pistol, opened the middle drawer of his desk, and dropped it in. Having locked the drawer, he filled a pipe and lit it, wondering what he should do. Whoever had put the pistol here expected him to do something. Telephone the police? Doubtless that is what he should do. He knew little of guns, but he was reasonably certain that this was a .22. Such a gun had been used in the killing of Enoch Hingle as well as of Stevie O'Brien. But who would have the desire, let alone the opportunity, to lay the weapon on the desk of the pastor of St. Hilary's?

He tried to imagine the person who had come to the door of his study, crossed the carpet, and placed the weapon on his desk. This had happened during the past half hour. It might have been only minutes ago. The deed sought to make him the accomplice of some plan, and he did not like that. But the gun might have been put here as a plea for help, help of the kind only a priest could give.

Father Dowling put on his coat, relit the pipe that in his distraction he had not properly lighted in the first place, and tried the front door. It was not locked. He opened it and stepped onto the porch and his eye was drawn toward the school. Clouds formed in front of his face whether or not he held the pipe in his mouth. Cold. He went down the steps and onto the sidewalk shoveled clean by Feeney and started toward the school, head down. Was he shielding himself from the wind or looking for footprints, some telltale trace. Foolish. Besides, the walk was too clean to record anyone's passage along it.

Standing in the doorway of the school gymnasium, Roger Dowling looked in at the old people, hard at work having fun, passing the time, diverting themselves from the realization that they required diversion to make themselves less of a burden to themselves and those who loved them. From the far end of the room Edna Hospers waved to him, indicating that she would be with him in a moment. While he waited for her, Roger Dowling looked at Jennie Carr playing checkers with a white-haired man. She had just made her move and now sat back, smiling triumphantly at her opponent. He brooded over the board, ignoring her. The priest went to stand beside the couple.

"Good afternoon, Father," Jennie said brightly.

Roger Dowling returned the greeting. Carlo Liberati looked up at the priest, nodded, then returned to planning his move.

Jennie said, "Have you found any more bodies, Father?"

"Have any been lost?"

Jennie giggled in appreciation. Carlo Liberati made his move.

When Edna came up, Roger Dowling walked her into the hall. "Are you busy, Edna? Of course you are, but can you spare a minute?"

"Is something wrong?"

"Not that I know of. Let's go to your office." As they walked down the hallway he said, "Tell me, Edna. Has Jennie Carr been behaving herself lately?"

"Well, she hasn't locked me in any more closets."

"That tells me what she hasn't been doing."

Edna sighed. "I try to tell myself it's just her odd sense of humor, but it really doesn't help."

"Has she got these old men doing any more foolish things?"

"No, thank God."

"The man she's playing checkers with doesn't look as if he would be putty in her hands."

"Carlo? They are a pair, those two. Thick as thieves.

Not that he takes part in her antics. She put honey into the sweeping compound and poor Feeney took a handful to scatter on the floor and it was an hour before he got his hands clean."

"You're sure Jennie did it?"

"It's only an educated guess. I didn't accuse her of it. I don't think I could face her daughter again if Jennie does something seriously mischievous."

"That would be Evelyn Cunningham?"

"Then I mentioned her to you."

"I've heard of her."

He had heard of her from Phil Keegan, who had come to the rectory last night and brought Roger Dowling up to date on the investigation of the killings of Enoch Hingle and Stevie O'Brien. Iggie O'Brien, now that his son was buried, had escalated his demands that the police find his son's killer.

"I called Martin and told him it was his responsibility to calm down his father. If we have to, we'll tell Iggie what Stevie was involved in, but I'd rather not. Of course, if we ever solve those damned murders the truth will come out."

"If?"

Keegan looked miserable. "Roger, we are chasing phantoms. Poor Horvath. He had a talk with Liberati's secretary and she as much as said her boss is in the drug trade. Horvath thinks Hingle and Stevie made the mistake of poaching on Liberati's territory and paid the price."

"That sounds plausible."

"It is. But we need evidence. Liberati was in his secretary's apartment the night Stevie was killed. He says he was with his father, but we know different. Either way, it's of no help."

"His secretary?"

"A floozy named Charmaine." Keegan described the woman with evident distaste.

"She is the *young* Liberati's secretary?"

"That's right. Then Horvath drove out to Liberati's marina and found a woman on the dock, all alone, an old girl friend of Liberati's. Evelyn Cunningham. Her mother spends her days here at your parish center."

"What's her name?"

Keegan dug out a notebook and flipped through it. "Jennifer Carr. Roger, why do I have that name written down here? You can see how desperate we are."

When they arrived at Edna's office, Roger Dowling closed the door after them. This surprised Edna a little. She went behind her desk and sat down. Roger Dowling remained on his feet, looking out the window at the parish house. It had taken him a minute and a half, walking slowly, to get from the house to the school gym.

"Edna, I have a strange question. Did any of your old people leave the gym during the past fifteen minutes?"

She laughed. "Probably half the men. They go to the lavatory incessantly. Why?"

"Any women?"

"I really couldn't say. I don't keep that close a watch on them. Is something wrong?"

"I told you it was a strange question. I'm wondering if one of them could have gone over to the parish house during the past quarter hour."

Edna thought about it, but her expression did not suggest that she would be able to remember.

Father Dowling said, "Did Jennie Carr leave the gym? Or perhaps Carlo Liberati?"

"What has she been up to, Father?"

"Edna, I can't explain why I'm asking. Given the way Jennie has been behaving, wouldn't you have noticed if she had gone out?"

"Father, why don't you just ask her?"

"Would she tell me the truth?"

Edna considered that for a moment. She shook her head. "I doubt it. Can't you tell me what's wrong?"

"It's most likely only a tempest in a teapot."

She was a puzzled woman when he left her, but he could not burden her with the knowledge of the pistol that had been left on his desk. Back in his study, he unlocked the drawer of his desk and, using the pipe knife, again lifted the pistol so he could examine the barrel. The name was there, elegantly scrolled. Carlo Liberati. He locked it up in the drawer again, lit a pipe, and sat there, puffing and thinking.

St. Hilary's no longer seemed on the periphery of the case Phil Keegan and Cy Horvath were working on. The truck with Enoch Hingle's body might have been abandoned anywhere, so the fact that it had been left beside the rectory in itself meant nothing. But the presence of Carlo Liberati and of Jennie Carr, the mother of Evelyn Cunningham, and the fact that Charmaine, the secretary at the Liberati used-car lot, called for Carlo at the end of the day, went beyond the bounds of coincidence. And now the .22 pistol reported missing by Rob Liberati had shown up on his desk. Was it the murder weapon he had locked in his drawer?

Roger Dowling picked up the phone and put through a call to Phil Keegan, but he was not available. Neither was Horvath. The priest said he would call back later. He left his name. He did not want Phil to think he had delayed letting him know of this startling development.

During the afternoon the day turned bright and sunny, the temperature rose to an unseasonable level, and the sound of dripping water as icicles melted from the eaves was background music to Roger Dowling's pondering. At four Phil had not yet called and Roger Dowling was about to telephone him again when Marie Murkin burst into the study, flourishing a jar of jelly, a triumphant look on her face.

"Look what I found!"

"Strawberry or raspberry?"

"Father, it's one of the stolen jars! They were buried in the snow in the backyard. I noticed something shiny in the sunlight when I came from the store and this is what it was. The rest of them were buried deeper, but they were all there. And the pork chops too."

He went with her into the backyard to see where the treasure had been buried. Marie obviously regarded the mystery as solved and he did not encourage her to wonder who had buried her preserves in the snow. As he stood there he looked toward the street, to where the stolen truck with Enoch Hingle's body had been parked. There were old footprints in the snow, sunken and blurred now in the heat of the sun, all but indistinct. He and Mrs. Murkin had walked across the yard through the snow to the truck, but that did not account for one set of tracks that came at an angle from the sidewalk parallel to the street.

Fooling with his pipe, adopting a distracted air, Roger Dowling strolled up the walk to the church, followed the walk to the front of the church, and then came down the public sidewalk. As he walked he studied the pattern of footprints in the snow. It was relatively easy to make out the path he and Marie Murkin had made when they went out to the truck. The indentations he had noticed earlier were quite distinct from these. They went to a spot in the yard and then returned to the sidewalk. Roger Dowling stepped into the melting footprints and followed them to where they stopped. There he crouched and began to feel around in the snow. Nothing. He looked over his shoulder. He was not directly opposite from where the stolen truck had been, but at a point perhaps ten yards in front of it.

He was opposite where the second truck would have been, the one that had towed the stolen truck.

Suddenly Father Dowling straightened and walked directly toward the house, going at a purposeful pace to the back door, not minding at all that the wet slushy snow dampened his shoes and socks. Inside the kitchen, he opened the basement door and started down.

He found Feeney behind the furnce, tipped back in a chair wedged between the furnace and the wall, sound asleep.

"Feeney," he said, keeping his voice low. "Feeney." He reached over to shake the man awake, but all it took was a touch on the arm and the janitor sat forward, startled but awake.

"Where is the pistol, Feeney?"

"I don't have it!"

If he had had more time, if he had been fully awake, Feeney might not have answered the question. Or he might have answered falsely. Father Dowling let out his breath in relief.

"Of course you don't. You put it on my desk. Why?"

Feeney struggled to his feet and came out from behind the furnace. Awake now, he was belatedly on his guard. "I don't know what you're talking about."

"Feeney, you found a pistol in the backyard. I know that. And you know what I'm talking about. Why did you put it on my desk?"

"I didn't! Honest to God, Father. I didn't put anything on your desk."

"Someone did it for you?"

"No. Look, you're right. I found the gun. I put it my room. Don't ask me why."

Roger Dowling shook his head. "Not good enough, Feeney. When Father Rabb was here he took the liberty of searching your room. I objected to that, but he was in there and going through your things before I realized what he was doing. He didn't find a gun. Believe me, he would have if it was there."

"But it wasn't there then. Someone took it."

"Come upstairs, Feeney. You and I are going to have a long talk."

"In confidence?"

"How do you mean?"

"You're a priest. What I tell you you can't tell anyone else, right?"

"Not quite. You're thinking of confession. Do you want to go to confession?"

Thoughts fled across Feeney's face like clouds in a storm. Finally he shook his head. "No. But I'll only talk in confidence."

"Feeney, if you have committed some crime, I can't keep that secret."

"But I haven't done anything wrong. I mean it. I haven't."

"Then you have nothing to fear. Come on, let's go upstairs."

Roger Dowling knew as he pieced together Feeney's story, extracting it from the terrified ex-con a fragment at a time, and then gaining Feeney's eager assent to his own connected narrative, that Phil Keegan would never believe it. He told Feeney as much.

"Father, leave me out of it. Give him the gun. It was just a lucky guess and tricking me that let you find out. Cops are used to mysteries. The main thing they want is the weapon."

"You should have thought of that when you found it."

"I didn't want to get involved."

Roger Dowling could not tell Feeney that he might have succeeded in that if he had not decided to put the gun on the study desk. Feeney had done it out of fear. A gun that had been missing was suddenly back in his drawer. Knowing what it had once been used for, he was certain it had been used to kill Stevie O'Brien. Someone was trying to set him up.

"Who?"

"How the hell should I know?"

Was this only more caution? It was difficult to believe that Feeney had not noticed the name engraved on the barrel of the gun. The one thing Dowling was sure of was that Feeney's prints weren't on it.

When Phil called, Roger Dowling told him he had the pistol Rob Liberati had reported missing. He watched Feeney as he said this, but the little janitor did not blink an eye. See no evil, hear no evil. Not that he was not paying attention to the conversation. As soon as he knew it was the police, he came to the edge of his chair.

"Don't kid me, Roger," Phil said. "I'm not in the mood."

"I'm serious. Someone left it on my desk this afternoon."

After a pause Phil said, "I'm coming out."

After he had hung up, Roger Dowling looked at Feeney. The little man stared bird-like at him, not breathing, waiting. It was a most difficult moment for Roger Dowling. Phil Keegan would find Feeney's story fantastic, but Roger Dowling was certain it was true. And, if it was true, the alternative that suggested itself seemed more fantastic still. Roger Dowling did not relish the thought of deceiving his old friend, but neither did he wish to jeopardize Feeney's freedom by involving him in a murder investigation. Innocent Feeney might be, but he had acted stupidly.

"You'd better go back to work, Feeney. You won't want to be here when I talk with Captain Keegan."

"Are you going to tell him?"

"I am going to tell him that I found this pistol on my desk."

"That's all?"

"For now, yes."

Feeney stood before the desk, wringing his hands, and there were tears in his eyes. "Thanks, Father. I'll never forget this."

"I can't promise that I won't have to tell him, Feeney. That depends on lots of things."

"Once they have the gun, they'll find the ones who did it."

"According to your story, they already have arrested them."

"They'll figure it out, Father."

Roger Dowling wished he shared Feeney's confidence in the police's ability to solve a crime when important information about the murder weapon was withheld from them. After Feeney had scuttled from the office, Roger Dowling resolved not to keep Phil Keegan in the dark longer than he had to. His justification for what he meant to do involved more people than Feeney and Phil Keegan. But he did not yet know precisely who they were.

Some minutes later, standing at his window, Roger Dowling looked up the street to where the old people were coming out of the school, as if they had been transported back to the student days of the first decade of their lives. Jennie Carr and Carlo Liberati stood at the curb, arm in arm. Odd. A car pulled up and they both got in. Roger Dowling could not remember ever seeing them leave together before. It was Carlo's habit to get into the car driven by the blonde.

There was no sign of the blonde or her car in the street.

30

CARLO LIBERATI was worried. On one of his trips to the john, leaving Jennie the chance to rearrange the pieces on the board, he had gone to Feeney's room to get the gun. When he had told Jennie to put it back where she found it, he had not been thinking too straight. He should have taken it out to the end of the dock and pitched it into the river. Without it, no case in the Hingle or O'Brien killings could be proved. The idea that returning it to Feeney's room would put things back to where they had been didn't wash. But when he went into Feeney's room and checked out the dresser drawer, he could not find the 22.

He went through all the drawers of the dresser systematically, having locked the door of the room. He took the bed apart. He looked in every conceivable hiding place. Nothing. He stood with his back to the locked door and studied the room.

There was no sign that it had been searched. Small comfort. Where the hell was the gun?

He thought of two possibilities. Feeney, surprised to find the gun back, had gotten rid of it himself. The fact that he had not raised any hell about it's being missing indicated that he knew something of the history of the gun. Carlo went to the window of the room and saw the view it gave of the street where Hingle's body had been found. Had Feeney witnessed the abandoning of the truck?

There was another possibility. Jennie could have kept the gun. He had seen her take it into Feeney's room but he hadn't looked through her purse afterward to make sure she had left the gun in the dresser. On the whole, Carlo thought the second possibility the more likely.

"I thought you fell in," Jennie said when he came back to the gym. A glance at the board told Carlo she had been altering the pieces in his absence. She was an inveterate cheater at checkers. And probably everything else.

"I ran into Feeney."

"It's your move."

The name got no particular reaction from her. Carlo sat and lost the game and bided his time. It was late in the afternoon before he got a chance to look in Jennie's purse. The gun was not there. If she had kept it, she must have taken it home. He had to find out.

"Your daughter coming for you tonight?"

Jennie sighed. "Who else?"

"I need a ride."

Jennie frowned in thought. "I don't know. Evelyn is an odd woman."

"I know Evelyn."

"My daughter Evelyn? How could you?"

"She used to come to the marina."

"And you remember her?"

"Since I met you. I put two and two together."

Jennie did not seem to know what to think of that. Well, Carlo knew what Jennie thought of her daughter. He could have matched any of her stories with stories about Roberto, but why bother? Until it was time to go, Jennie was quiet, as if she was trying to figure out some way of keeping Carlo from seeing her daughter. She slipped away and got her coat on early, but Carlo was watching and he caught up with her as she was trying to get the street door open. He put his own hand against it and it opened.

"I thought you had a bad heart."

"My arm's all right."

He gave her his arm as they walked out to the street, and the gesture reconciled her to his determination to bum a ride with Evelyn. When they got out to the street and were waiting on the curb, Carlo looked down the street to where Charmaine was parked. Even if she saw him, she would wait there. He didn't care if she saw him or not. It would do her good to cool her heels and then find he wasn't coming. Jennie tried to tug her arm free and Carlo took hold of Jennie's thin wrist with his other hand. A car had drawn up at the curb. The driver's window rolled down and there was Evelyn smiling up at him.

"Mr. Liberati! How are you?"

Carlo smiled but it was not in recognition. He searched the heavily made-up face for some reminder of the past and could not find any.

"Carlo wants a ride," Jennie said.

Evelyn could not have been more pleased. They sat three in the front seat, Carlo in the middle, Jennie silent on his right and Evelyn a gushing girl behind the wheel, telling him how well she remembered summer days at the marina. Why, she had actually gone out there a few days ago, for old time's sake.

"You shoulda come by the house."

"Is that where you want to go now?"

"Gotta fix my supper."

"You cook for yourself!"

"If you can call it that." Carlo prided himself on his cooking ability, and with reason, but to brag about it now was no way to get to Jennie's place.

"Come eat with us. Jennie, wouldn't that be nice? Mr. Liberati for dinner."

"Only if he's well done," Jennie said, then giggled and dug an elbow into Carlo's rib. It gave him an excuse to lean against Evelyn and then they all laughed at Jennie's joke.

It was an apartment, not a house, and he was glad of that. His offer to help make the meal was dismissed as another joke; they shooed him off to watch television and he asked where the bathroom was. What had to be Jennie's room was just beyond the bathroom. He turned on the bathroom light, pulled the door closed from the outside and went into Jennie's room. On that first trip, he went through her dresser, patting down the clothes, encountering no gun. He went out and diddled with the television, looked into the kitchen, and was again told to go relax. The second time, he checked out the closet, running his hands down the dresses and sweaters, feeling about on the shelf. Nothing. He was beginning to doubt his theory. At table, it turned out that just finding the gun would not be enough.

"What's this Jennie tells me about you two stealing a gun?" Evelyn asked, looking at Carlo as she might a naughty boy.

"I don't know. What did she tell you?"

"I didn't tell her nothing," Jennie said.

"You mean you told me a lie?"

"Think what you like."

The bad news had an oddly positive effect on Carlo's

appetite and he launched into the minute steak with relish. So both of them would know that a .22 stolen from Feeney's room had been in Carlo Liberati's possession for days. Things were more complicated than he had thought. He would have to un-complicate them. Too bad. But, the topic having been raised, he could discuss it freely.

"Did you put it back where you got it?" he asked Jennie.

Jennie lowered her brow and darted her eyes at Evelyn. Secrets.

"Were you two really fooling around with a gun?"

"It wasn't in Feeney's room," Carlo said to Jennie.

"I put it there. You saw me. I know you were watching."

"What in heaven's name would you want with a gun? And why would the janitor at Saint Hilary's have one in his room?"

Carlo shrugged. Her questions did not bother him. Others would occur to her soon enough. She would remember the killings. Too bad. It really was too bad. After the first shock of seeing Evelyn as a middle-aged woman, Carlo had come to see that she had an attractiveness appropriate to her present age. Jennie and Evelyn. Mother and daughter. It was a damned shame, but it was their fault, not his. He could not let the two of them walk around with the knowledge that he had had that .22 in his possession when Stevie O'Brien had been killed.

31

PHIL KEEGAN had been on his way out of the office on his way to Roger Dowling's when he ran into Cy Horvath and Agnes Lamb, the black woman cop.

"Agnes has found out something, Captain. The way Stevie O'Brien's body got out to that ice fishing shack."

Keegan stopped. Agnes's expression was impassive and her eyes took him in as if anxious to catch his reaction. That was the damnable thing about the woman; she made him feel that he and the whole department were on some kind of trial and she was their judge. His impulse was to take Cy with him, leave Agnes, and beat it out to Dowling's. He inhaled deeply, expanding his chest, and turned back into his office.

"Let's hear it."

He was glad he decided to hear it now, and from Agnes.

She recited the tale like a kid in school and could not keep out of her voice the sense that she had come up with something truly important. Keegan didn't blame her. Maybe Cy was right and the woman could become a halfway decent cop after all.

"Charmaine Hegel? The woman who works for Liberati?"

"Lieutenant Horvath told me to check her out."

Keegan looked at Cy.

"She was too helpful, Captain, blowing the whistle on Liberati as if she didn't know what she was doing."

Keegan looked back at Agnes, who still stood more or less at attention. He told her to sit down. She preferred to stand. Keegan felt that he had been corrected in some subtle way, he did not know how. But his pique at Agnes disappeared soon enough.

Charmaine Hegel had connections in Chicago with the mob, passed from hand to hand as companion, but obviously something more than just another dumb blonde. She had managed a bar, she had acted as buyer for a boutique that necessitated frequent trips East during which she had acted as an emissary for her silent partners. Just when it seemed she was destined for apparent legitimacy, the better to serve her real bosses, she had been sent to Fox River with Albini, Gruening, and DiNigro.

"Summoned," Horvath corrected.

Agnes nodded. "Right."

"By Liberati?"

"Carlo Liberati," Agnes said, consulting her notes. "The father. She was carrying on with both him and the son. She was entertaining the son the night Stevie O'Brien was killed. That made me think. So I checked out her car. There was a large sheet of plastic in the trunk, folded up, not very clean. I brought it to the lab."

"The preliminary examination turned up blood," Cy said. "The car has been impounded."

Agnes said, having listened impatiently when Horvath interrupted, "I am betting that Stevie O'Brien's body was transported in that car."

"Woman's intuition?" Keegan said, annoyed at the tone of his own voice.

Agnes looked at him for a moment, then shook her head. "No. Training. Routine."

Keegan stood and came around the desk. Agnes drew herself taller and her chin lifted. Keegan put a hand on her arm and felt her stiffen.

"Good work, Lamb. Damned good work. Let's go to the lab."

Solomon was as sure as Lamb now. The blood stains on the plastic sheet matched Stevie O'Brien's.

"Bring her in," Keegan snapped.

"I did," Agnes said. "She resisted and I had to get a little rough. But she is booked and in a cell."

Keegan allowed himself to smile. When he patted Agnes Lamb's arm this time, she did not stiffen.

"I like that. Action."

"Affirmative action," Agnes purred, and there was a slightly taunting look in her eyes.

"Yeah. Come on, you two. We're going out to Saint Hilary's. Roger Dowling called to tell me he has the murder weapon."

There had been other times when Roger Dowling had annoyed Phil Keegan, but this was the worst. His old friend expected him to believe that a .22 pistol had mysteriously appeared on his desk top and he hadn't the faintest idea where it had come from. Two minutes after they got there, Agnes was on her way back downtown with the weapon. Keegan wanted Solomon to check it out. When the call came from the lab, Dowling was still sticking to his fairy tale about how the weapon had come into his possession. Keegan put down the phone.

"Okay. You're right, Roger. That is the weapon. It was used to kill Enoch Hingle and it was used to kill Stevie O'Brien. Now, let's quit horsing around. Try guessing where the gun came from."

Horvath said, "Carlo Liberati spends his days here at the parish center."

Leave it to Horvath to find the link. Keegan nodded. "Go get him, Cy."

"Should I bring him here?"

"No!" Keegan glared at Roger Dowling. "Take him downtown."

Dowling busied himself with his pipe, and Keegan, furious with his old friend, stalked out to the kitchen to get a beer from the refrigerator. From upstairs came the murmur of Marie Murkin's television. Back in the study, Keegan sank into a chair and took a long drink from his beer. Dowling spoke from a cloud of smoke.

"Phil, just between the two of us now, let me tell you how the gun got here. Just listen and promise me you won't do the first thing that comes into your mind."

"I'll listen, Roger. No more."

"The man who put the gun on my desk has the best reason in the world not to be involved with the police."

"Feeney!"

"Feeney. That's right. I warn you, the story sounds fantastic."

Fantastic was the word for it. Listening, Phil Keegan wondered if Roger Dowling believed the story himself. Feeney had witnessed the abandonment of the truck. He had seen three men. When they drove away, they had thrown something into the snowy yard. The following day, Feeney had waded through the snow and retrieved the .22, which he had then stashed in his room, knowing it was evidence in a capital crime. And then the gun was missing.

"When?"

"The period coincides with the murder of Stevie O'Brien."

"Convenient."

"Well, significant. It *was* missing, Phil."

Roger Dowling told of Cletus Rabb's search of Feeney's room. At least Rabb had the sense to distrust Feeney. Keegan said as much but Roger Dowling ignored it. The gun showed up again, right where it had been before, and Feeney was scared, very scared. That is when he decided to put the burden on Father Dowling.

"You believe all that?"

"Yes." The priest puffed on his pipe. "Why not? I know Feeney had nothing to do with the death of Stevie O'Brien. He had no motive."

"Maybe he was given an assignment he couldn't turn down."

"Cletus Rabb is certain that murder is not in Feeney's line. Cy's guess is the right one, Phil."

Carlo Liberati? Well, Keegan couldn't deny this made a lot more sense. Liberati was related by blood to the killings. The gun that had killed Hingle and Stevie O'Brien bore his signature. Keegan finished his beer.

"I want to see Feeney."

"He can't tell you anything more than I've told you, Phil. Can't you leave him out of this? He is genuinely terrified to become known as someone who helped the police."

"If he saw those men leave the truck here, he is going to have to be a witness."

"Can't we wait and see if that's true? Phil, I promised him."

The phone rang. The priest answered it and then passed it to Keegan. It was Cy Horvath.

"He's not at home, Captain."

"Who is?"

"No one."

"You inside?"

"Yes."

Keegan thought. "Find him. Cy? Bring in Robbie too."

He hung up the phone. Roger Dowling suggested he have another beer. It seemed as good an idea as any. Roger might have promised Feeney, but Phil Keegan was making no promises. Yet it would do no harm to have another bottle of beer before he decided whether or not to bounce Feeney around. If nothing else, he wanted to hear this story again, but from the horse's whatchamacallit.

32

FATHER DOWLING had commended the murder of Enoch Hingle to Marcus Riehle's novelist's imagination to see what his literary capacity might dream up as an explanation. But Marcus Riehle had always relied on facts rather than imagination. That Evelyn Cunningham had been surprised standing on the dock at the Liberati marina was a fact. It was also a fact that, years ago, she had been an object of attention both of Liberati *père* and Liberati *fils*. Or should he say *padre* and *figlio?*

Marcus Riehle made the same pilgrimage to the scene of his youthful anguish and frustration. How unchanged it seemed. Parked on the road at the wheel of his Jeepster he looked out at the wintry beach and the sounds of summer seemed to drift to him across the snow-covered sand. The writer needs a sense of place every bit as much as he who meditates according to the method of St. Ignatius. When he drove away,

Marcus felt prepared to confront the woman Evelyn had become.

Madness is method. He rose at an ungodly hour and parked his Jeepster down the street from the entrance to the building where Evelyn lived in an apartment with her aged mother. He waited an hour before they emerged and drove off to St. Hilary's. Marcus followed at a discreet distance but in truth he felt invisible. It was as if his memory and imagination alone were at work, he and the Jeepster unreal. The glimpse he had gotten of Evelyn sufficed to re-create the tantalizing woman of so many summers ago.

At St. Hilary's parish center, the little old woman got out of the car and tottered to the door of the school. Evelyn waited until her mother was safely inside before driving away. During that moment, Marcus felt his heart go out to Evelyn. This devotion to her mother spoke well of the woman who had once wrung his heart. He could dismiss the thought that she had married three times and on one painful occasion suffered Carlo Liberati to take her in his arms in the boathouse. The marriages seemed momentarily as trivial as that girlish indiscretion.

Marcus followed Evelyn across town to the architecture firm where she was employed as a receptionist. There was a restaurant across the street in which Marcus had his belated breakfast and then lingered over coffee for more than an hour. He ran the motor of his Jeepster when he went back to it, so he could have the heater on. At eleven, he got out of the Jeepster, crossed to the architect's office, and entered. Evelyn turned an impersonal smile upon him. Marcus opened his mouth and no words came out.

He stood there, his mouth working, his eyes looking wild, trying unsuccessfully to speak. When he fled he thanked God Evelyn had not recognized him.

Back in his Jeepster, he felt with the keenness of a long-ago summer that in Evelyn's eyes he simply did not exist. But why should he think his stock would rise with the passage of time? Depression at being unrecognized—worse than rejection—gave way to anger. It was ludicrous to seek the favor of Evelyn Cunningham. The woman was a worse failure at life than Marcus Riehle. Imagine the effect three failures at marriage must have on her self-esteem. And he must not forget that Evelyn had cavorted with both Rob Liberati and his father years ago.

The sun had come out and the temperature rose and with it Marcus's spirit as he reminded himself of his original purpose for looking up Evelyn after all these years. It was stupid to think his motive had been to reactivate an imaginary relationship. With the eye of imagination he was to look at the few facts he knew and construct a plausible account of the death of Enoch Hingle. And of Stevie O'Brien. Father Dowling had provided Evelyn's link with those deaths. First of all, the site, St. Hilary's, where Evelyn's aged mother spent her days, brought there by Evelyn. Second, the presence at St. Hilary's of Carlo Liberati too. Had the incongruous embrace he had witnessed long ago in the boathouse been renewed?

Evelyn Cunningham, vixen, voracious consumer of men—he could imagine her renewing that old acquaintance, despite Carlo's age. Would that not appeal to her perversity? Of course, an old man could not satiate her; there would have been others as well. The fact that young Liberati had reported a .22 missing with "Carlo Liberati" engraved on it connected the old man with the killings, at least in the imagination of a novelist manqué. And then Marcus thought he had it. He would stake his reputation as a writer on the hunch that Evelyn had been carrying on with the two dead men, with Enoch Hingle and Stevie O'Brien. And Carlo Liberati had killed them both.

Marcus Riehle tried the story from various angles and

any way he looked at it it seemed good to him. In the street the snow was turning to slush in the sunlight. He rolled down his window and the slurpy sound of traffic pleased him, a premature spring to greet the imaginative discovery he had made.

At noon Evelyn emerged, stood on the walk for a moment, looking indecisively up and down the street before walking toward the corner. Marcus hopped out of the Jeepster and began walking up the street in the same direction, but on the opposite side. Evelyn turned the corner and Marcus ran to the intersection but the light was red and he could not cross. For a moment he did not see Evelyn and he stamped his feet, impatient for the light to change. Before it did, he saw her. And then she disappeared, into the entrance of a restaurant.

Marcus crossed on green and walked past the restaurant, not even looking in. Several doors past, he stopped. The thought of lunch brought on hunger, but the restaurant Evelyn had entered was the only one around. He could not enter it unless he meant to approach her. She might not remember the Marcus Riehle of years ago but she would remember the strange man who had stood before her desk, unable to speak, and who had fled without a word.

So he waited on the walk. Tires in the melting snow made a curious sound, water dripped from the ledge above him. He stepped into the doorway and then realized it was a tavern. It might have been a haven if Marcus were a drinking man. He was not. Several of his pamphlets had dealt with intemperance but he had written them from the same distant and theoretical viewpoint from which he wrote of marriage. From time to time the door of the tavern opened and along with the stale smell of beer came the aroma of hamburgers. Salivating, Marcus resisted the lure for five minutes. There was no reason to fear that he would lose the trail of Evelyn Cunningham. If she finished her lunch quickly, she would return to work. It was the thought of the long afternoon before she would return to St. Hilary's to pick up her mother that decided Marcus. He needed food. He had to keep up his strength.

Inside, the tavern was full of smoke and men and noise, but the important thing was the smell of food. The few tables and booths at the front were occupied and the bar was thick with customers. Marcus continued into the lively yet somehow gloomy place and came into a back portion where there were more tables, several free, and a harried waitress.

Marcus took off his coat and hung it over the back of a chair and sat. The plastic-coated menu contained a surprising variety of greasy delights, but Marcus's problem was not so much one of selection as pronunciation. His experience when he confronted Evelyn indicated that his old impediment had returned after a brief dramatic freedom from it. Sitting in the Jeepster he could, of course, talk to himself, even talk aloud, but stuttering occurred only when he addressed others. So too now, in his mind, he could easily form the phrase "A burger and beer," but the prospect of trying to negotiate those explosive labials after he had caught the attention of the waitress filled him with dread. And then she was beside him, looking exhausted and distracted, asking what his would be.

Marcus pointed at the menu.

"A hamburger?"

He nodded.

She looked at him. "What do you want on it?"

"Everything." The word floated free and he could have cried out with relief.

"A beer?"

"A d-d-d. . ." But he could not say it.

"A draft? Right."

And she was gone. The trivial little drama seemed to sum up his life. The elation he had felt at coming up with a sce-

nario for the murders of two men had been as nothing compared with his ability to say "Everything" to the waitress. And
that triumph had turned to shame when he could not get past
the d in draft. The reappearance of the waitress filled him with
fear of the renewal of shame.

"Rare all right for that burger?"

Marcus detested meat that was not well done but he
nodded eagerly and she went away. It seemed a small victory to
offset defeat, but his spirit struggled and began to rise.

The burger was inedible and the beer was awful. He ate
a third of the one and took several medicinal sips of the other
and was out of the tavern before ten minutes had elapsed.
Waiting again for Evelyn to come out of the restaurant, he was
bothered by the realization that she might have left while he
was suffering in the tavern. He could go back to his Jeepster. He
didn't. He waited and eventually Evelyn emerged, walked
briskly back to her office, Marcus following on the opposite side
of the street. He spent the next four hours and a half behind the
wheel of his parked Jeepster.

When he followed Evelyn's car to St. Hilary's and
watched her pick up her mother and a man he knew instantly to
be Carlo Liberati, Marcus was convinced his theory was veri-
fied. The mismatched couple had reconciled after Carlo had
gotten rid of his rivals. Certainty increased when Carlo went
into Evelyn's apartment building with the two women. Marcus
parked across the street and continued a vigil the exact significance of which he could not have expressed.

With the return of hunger came the resolution to insert
himself into the theory he had concocted. He would present
himself at the door of Evelyn's apartment and . . . And what?
Given this new task, he ignored the protests of his stomach and
put his novelist's imagination to work.

33

FEENEY, summoned by Phil Keegan and escorted by Mrs. Murkin, cast a betrayed look at Roger Dowling when he came into the study. The housekeeper had something of the aspect of a turnkey as she took up a position in the doorway and glared at him. Marie seemed to think that all her suspicions of the little janitor were going to be proved true.

"Marie," Father Dowling said, "would you bring Mr. Feeney a bottle of beer?"

Feeney and Marie Murkin reacted with different modalities of surprise to this, Feeney's doubled by the prospect of beer and being referred to so formally.

"I'll have another too, Marie," Phil Keegan said.

That she was waiting on Phil Keegan too made it easier for Marie and she scooted away. Feeney, who had slumped into a chair, sat straighter now. He crossed one leg over the other and studied the books behind Phil Keegan. His effort to look casual was a failure, not least because Phil Keegan said nothing while he waited for his beer and Roger Dowling did not want to speak lest he give Feeney further reason to think he had been betrayed by the pastor of St. Hilary's. But soon the beer was served, Marie Murkin, at Keegan's suggestion, had withdrawn, and Feeney faced his Torquemada.

All in all he did well, Roger Dowling thought, but then, this was not a maiden performance. How often had Feeney hunkered down to the task of not quite answering the probing questions of police?

"Yeah," he said in summary. "I found it where I said. I put it in my room. Someone took it, then put it back. That's when I put it on the Father's desk."

Keegan's efforts to extract motivations for any of the actions in that sequence were in vain. Feeney left the impression of a mechanical man, unthinkingly doing the things he related.

"And you saw three men leave the truck with Hingle's body in it?"

Feeney reluctantly nodded.

"So by the time you picked up the gun, you knew about Hingle and you would have guessed the gun had a connection with his murder?"

Fenney's head rocked slowly from left to right, he puffed out his lower lip, raised his brows, and shrugged.

"You knew," Keegan told him. "Okay. I don't have to tell you that is enough to return you to Joliet."

There was no visible reaction from Feeney. He was like a frame in a stopped film. Roger Dowling said, "You don't have to bring Feeney into this, Phil. You can connect the body and those three men without Feeney's testimony."

Keegan frowned. "I'm making no promises. That's all, Feeney. Scram."

Feeney scrammed, and soon after Phil Keegan did too, grumbling as he went that he wished Cy had found Carlo Liberati at his home.

He might have been leaving Roger Dowling with a point for meditation. When he saw the lights of Phil's car turn on in the street they seemed to illumine his mind as well as the window. He had stood there and watched Carlo Liberati and Jennie Carr being driven off together. Jennie. The antic old lady suddenly seemed a fitting prospect for the one who had entered Feeney's room and taken the pistol. It did not strain the imagination to think of her rummaging around in another's room. If she had taken the pistol, she would have shown it to Carlo Liberati, whose name was engraved on the barrel. Roger Dowling stopped puffing on his pipe. If she had taken it away, she would also have brought it back. Why? He could find no satisfactory answer to that question, but what did it matter, really, if he had indeed hit upon the way in which the pistol had disappeared and reappeared?

Roger Dowling opened the telephone directory, searched a page, and did not find the name of Jennie Carr. What was her daughter's name? He could not remember. He dialed Edna Hospers.

"She lives with her daughter," Edna said, and her voice was alive with curiosity. She must think that the pastor was obsessed with Jennie Carr. Well, that was not too far from the truth.

"What is her name, Edna?"

"Is this connected with this afternoon?"

Roger Dowling paused. "Yes. Don't ask me how, Edna. Please."

"Her name is Evelyn Cunningham."

He thanked Edna, wishing he could assuage her curiosity, but that was out of the question. If his suspicions were true, he did not know what it might mean.

Evelyn Cunningham was in the book. A moment's reflection convinced Roger Dowling that a telephone call would not do. He had to go to where Jennie lived.

He had some difficulty finding the street, but the building presented no problem at all. Both sides of the street were lined with parked cars. He found an empty space in front of a Jeepster. When he got out and closed the door the sound of it echoed oddly in the crisp winter air and, as he walked to the entrance, his shoes crackled on the icy concrete. He walked carefully, not wanting to slip and fall. Marie Murkin would have scolded him for not wearing his rubbers, if she knew. He had decided against telling the housekeeper he was going out. Mrs. Murkin was up in her room, watching television. Her day was done and it was highly unlikely that a parishioner would call in need of a priest. Besides, he did not expect to be gone long.

The street door of the apartment building was not locked. In the little lobby, Roger Dowling studied the rows of mailboxes inserted in the wall. Cunningham. 2A. That should put the apartment at the front of the building. He went outside again and looked up. The second-floor windows on both the right and left sides of the building were lighted. Roger Dowling went inside again and was surprised to find that the inner door too was unlocked. Not a very secure building.

The carpet on the stairs, florid and faded, was worn. A strange mixture of assorted sounds came muted to his ear as he mounted the stairs. The place was very warm and the air had a cooped-up smell, as if it had been used too many times. He reached the second floor and found himself at the door of 2A. He put an ungloved finger just above the bell and leaned toward the door until his ear was only inches from the panel.

Voices within, women's voices, and then another. A man's. He knocked and the voices stopped abruptly.

As one does when waiting for a door to be opened, Roger Dowling found himself deliberately arranging his expression but he had no prepared opening remark. A minute went by and the door had not opened nor had the voices resumed. He knocked again, insistently, and called through the door, "It's Father Dowling."

His voice sounded loud in the hall, but he could not tell if it had penetrated the door. Half a minute more went by before there was the sound of a chain being loosed. When the door opened Carlo Liberati looked out at Father Dowling. The priest's eyes went past the man to where the two women were seated on the couch, faces both frightened and hopeful, then dropped to the hand in which Carlo Liberati held a gun.

"Come in, Father," Carlo said. He stepped aside and Evelyn Cunningham burst into tears. Carlo's expression darkened and he beckoned with the gun. "Come on. Quick."

Roger Dowling went into the room, past Carlo. He heard the door close behind him and then the sound of the chain.

"Welcome to the excitement, Father," Jennie said, almost brightly. "Carlo, will you please put that popgun away. You know you're not going to shoot a priest and two women. That wouldn't make any sense at all."

Evelyn stared with wide tear-filled eyes at her mother. "Jennie, will you shut up?"

"Good idea," Carlo said, and Roger Dowling felt something hard press against his back. "Take a seat, Father."

"She's right, you know," Roger Dowling said, taking a pipe from his pocket as he sat down. It was better not to have the gun jabbing into his back. He looked up at Carlo Liberati, who no longer seemed quite so old. "I've come to have a talk with you, Mr. Liberati."

"Forget it."

"I wish I could. I wish *you* could. Unfortunately, it's a little late for that."

Evelyn's sobbing began again and Carlo looked at her impassively. The gun turned in her direction when he did and her sobbing became hysterical.

"Let the women leave the room," Roger Dowling said, marveling at the calmness of his own voice. How stupid he had been to walk into this situation. He had not even been surprised when Carlo opened the door with a gun in his hand. It was as though that was just what he had expected. On the other hand, he could not regret being able to come between the two women and an undoubtedly desperate man.

"We'll go to our rooms," Jennie said, and lifted herself to her feet. She took her daughter's hand. "Come on, my blubbering baby."

"Sit down," Carlo said.

Jennie ignored him and managed to tug Evelyn to her feet. They started out of the room and Roger Dowling spoke, to distract Carlo.

"Mr. Liberati, we don't have much time before the police get here."

Carlo ignored the women and studied Roger Dowling with hooded eyes for a moment. He shook his head. "A priest shouldn't lie."

"Why don't you give me that pistol? The police already have the other one. You must have quite an arsenal."

Silence followed, and it was difficult to tell from Carlo's manner whether he was worried. Then he walked slowly to the front windows and deliberately lowered the shades. Roger

Dowling thought of coming quickly up behind the old man and taking the pistol from him by force, but he remained in his chair. He realized that he recognized in Carlo Liberati a man who would use that gun.

Carlo turned from the now shaded windows and took a seat on the sofa vacated by Jennie and Evelyn. The sobbing of the daughter was audible still. Carlo rolled his tongue around the inside of his mouth and looked levelly at Roger Dowling.

"You shouldn't have come here. That was a mistake."

"Let's talk about your mistakes. Your sins, Carlo."

The old man's closed mouth widened in a grin and he looked defiantly at the priest. He shook his head. "Don't even start. It won't work."

"When did it stop working, Carlo? When did you stop thinking that God sees whatever you do."

"Maybe I never started."

"Oh, I doubt that. Maybe it would be better if I told you what happened, the events that led up to putting Stevie O'Brien's dead body in the trunk of Charmaine's car. You look surprised. When Jennie gave you the pistol she had found in Feeney's room, you recognized it of course. Your name was engraved on its barrel. You knew it was the weapon used to murder Enoch Hingle, a crime accomplished by the salesmen at your son's used-car lot."

"It's mine. I own it."

"The pistol?"

Carlo barked a disdainful laugh. "The lot."

"Your son was with Charmaine that night and ..." Something in Carlo's reaction made Roger Dowling pause. "Charmaine. She was arrested tonight, Carlo. She is in a cell at this very moment."

"You're lying." Carlo definitely reacted to the mention of the blonde Charmaine.

"The woman who came for you in the late afternoon at Saint Hilary's. The police know that her car was used to transfer the dead body of Stevie O'Brien to the lake where it was found. So they arrested her and put her in jail. I suppose you could say she is taking your place."

Carlo's mouth twitched and he glanced angrily in the direction of Evelyn Cunningham's crying, the sound of which was subsiding. Roger Dowling hoped there was a telephone in the room where the women were, but somehow he did not think so.

"Enoch Hingle was killed because he was interfering with the local drug trade. So was Stevie O'Brien. The police say the local trade was in your son's hands. As it had been in yours." Roger Dowling looked sadly at the sweatered, silver-haired man seated on the sofa with a gun in his hand. "Are you a seller of drugs, Carlo?"

"I kept the town clean."

"You shot Stevie O'Brien."

"So that's what you did with the gun, Carlo." It was Jennie, standing in the doorway, a taunting smile on her face. "No wonder you wanted it back." She came into the room and sat on the arm of the sofa, on the far end from Carlo. She shook her head and made a clicking sound. "How stupid you are."

"Go back to your room, Jennie," Roger Dowling advised.

"Oh, Carlo won't shoot me. He can't even beat me at checkers." She slid down onto the cushion of the couch, plucked a pillow propped in the corner, and put it demurely on her lap. "Give Father Dowling the gun, Carlo."

There was a sound of a knock at the door. Carlo sat forward and, as he did, Jennie threw the pillow at his head and scuttled along the sofa, her old woman's hand become a claw as she tried to get hold of the gun. Carlo rolled away from her and

Jennie shrieked, whether in fear or because of the excitement of the moment it would have been difficult to tell. There was a loud thump at the door and a grunting sound. A moment later there was another, the door crashed open, and Marcus Riehle came stumbling into the room. Carlo's arm lifted. He had pulled the trigger once before both Roger Dowling and Jennie flung themselves at him. The priest pinned the arm that held the gun and for an awful second realized it was pointing directly at his chest. With his other hand he grabbed the gun and directed it away from himself. It went off again, jolting his arm painfully, but then he wrested it free and it skidded across the room toward the fallen Marcus Riehle.

Roger Dowling moved swiftly, picking up the pistol and putting it into his pocket. It was then he realized Marcus had been hit. The fallen pamphleteer was groaning and clutching at his arm. Blood oozed through his fingers. Roger Dowling knelt beside him and Marcus's eyes rolled up at the priest.

"Is it just your arm, Marcus?"

The man nodded.

Roger Dowling spoke over his shoulder, "Jennie, telephone for an ambulance."

She started for the kitchen, then stopped. "The police too?"

Roger Dowling wished she didn't look so triumphant, making the arrest of Carlo Liberati some personal trick she was playing on her supposed friend. But then she deserved it, at least partly; she had acted like a heroine. Carlo Liberati sat on the couch, looking at the priest, seemingly disinterested in what had happened. Roger Dowling turned back to Marcus Riehle. He eased him onto his back.

"Th-th-tha . . ."

"Don't speak, Marcus. I understand."

34

THE TRIAL OF Gruening, Albini, and DiNigro was delayed indefinitely when one of the jurors reported to the judge that an attempt had been made to bribe her. Her accusation that others on the panel had succumbed to the temptation—she was quoting her tempter—opened a legal wrangle the outcome of which was still in doubt. Phil Keegan seemed remarkably philosophical about it as he sat in Roger Dowling's rectory. Perhaps the broadcast of a Cubs game in the Grapefruit League had something to do with it.

"All I do is catch them. The rest is up to the prosecutors." He took a sip of beer. "Thanks for your help, Roger." He said it grudgingly, and it was an apology, not praise. He had been furious with Roger Dowling for going to Evelyn Cunningham's apartment without informing him.

"It was only a guess that Carlo Liberati was there," Roger Dowling had said.

"You knew we were looking for him."

Roger Dowling let it go. His efforts to speak with Gruening, Albini, and DiNigro had been in vain. His failure with Carlo Liberati had not been total. For medical reasons the old man's trial had not been set. Carlo, his hospital bed cranked up, was watching television when the priest came into his private room. His lidded eyes dropped from the set perched high on the wall, then lifted again. The nut-brown skin and silver hair did not suggest illness, but Roger Dowling had talked with the nurse. However impassive the old man seemed, his heart had felt the strain of his deeds. At any moment Carlo Liberati could be transported to eternity. Seating himself beside the bed, Roger Dowling said this to Carlo.

"That's what they tell me."

The priest let a moment go by. "You must prepare yourself to meet God."

What had Thoreau replied to a similar remark in similar circumstances? Carlo Liberati was unlikely to claim to be on good terms with the Deity.

"You murdered Stevie O'Brien, Carlo."

Carlo pressed a button, turning off the television. He looked askance at the priest and his expression might have said that he had done more dreadful things than Roger Dowling could dream of.

"No charges will be brought against Charmaine. Or against your son."

Carlo shrugged.

"When did you last go to confession, Carlo?"

"Forget it, Father."

"That is what God offers to do, forget the sins we have committed. Think of your wife, Carlo. Think of your parents."

The conversation went on, the priest trying to find some wedge into the closed mind of the ailing murderer, some aperture through which divine mercy could enter. But the only hopeful thing was that Carlo did not order him from the room. He would come back, again and again, as often as it took. Phil Keegan heard about the visits and told Roger Dowling it was hopeless.

"He's been a hoodlum all his life, Roger. There isn't much he hasn't done."

"You should pray for him, Phil."

Phil Keegan's reaction vacillated between that of a Captain of Detectives and that of the former seminarian. "Yeah," he said.

On the radio, the Cubs went down in order and a commercial for a loan shark came on. Keegan lit a cigar and became an enigmatic figure in a cloud of blue smoke.

"Four murderers," he mused. "I'll bet we don't get a single conviction. We do a helluva lot better with traffic violations."

Roger Dowling understood his old friend's outlook without sharing it. It was a forlorn hope, the thought that justice will be done, all the loose ends tied up, the guilty punished, the innocent set free. The hunger and thirst for justice are not assuaged in this life.

"That makes crime more attractive than it is. I might take it up myself."

"We all have, Phil."

If Phil Keegan were going to be philosophical, it would be on his own terms. He knew what the priest meant, he believed it too, in a way, but not if it called into question the point of his own job. Justice and mercy, Roger Dowling thought, and he knew it was the second that is more important. Where would any of us be without it?

Marie Murkin came in with a bowl of popcorn and drove the subject away. She stood watching Phil Keegan go at it with a huge hand.

"Honestly," she said, shaking her head and looking around the study. The remark might have prefaced many things.

"What is it, Marie?"

She sighed. "Martha Ennis. That was her on the phone. I think she has a thing for Marcus Riehle. She sounds like a schoolgirl."

"Did Marcus address her group?"

"He was a triumph! I'm quoting. The woman is absolutely gaga. And now she's jealous."

"Jealous?"

"Marcus Riehle is seeing Evelyn Cunningham too."

Mrs. Murkin tried to look stern about all these shenanigans but despite herself she broke into a smile.

Phil Keegan paused in his munching. "You had your chance, Marie. Here you had Feeney with you day after day and you let him get away."

Marie Murkin, whose cap, as she would have put it, was set for Phil Keegan if it was set for anyone, looked pop-eyed at him. Her lips became a line and she breathed through her nose. Turning on her heel, she marched back to her kitchen. Phil grinned, unaware of what his kidding had done to Mrs. Murkin.

"It's too bad about Feeney, Roger."

"I wonder. Maybe he wanted to go back to prison. A man his age stealing an automobile simply for a joyride makes no sense. Besides, he had the use of my car whenever he wanted it."

"He did do one good thing on the outside," Keegan said through the mush of a half-masticated mouthful of popcorn. "Turning in that gun."

"That has to be kept a secret, Phil. His worst fear was that it would be found out he had been of help to the police."

Phil nodded. He understood. The two men sat in silence, half attending to the distant fortunes of the baseball team that regularly breaks the hearts of its fans. Was Feeney listening to the game in his cell at Joliet? Cletus Rabb had welcomed Feeney back. "The bird comes to love his cage, Roger," the prison chaplain said.

That might have applied to Cletus himself. Or to me, Roger Dowling thought, looking around the cluttered, smoke-filled, familiar study. From the kitchen came sounds of Marie Murkin banging around, the noise doubtless meant to carry to the study and annoy Phil Keegan. But the Captain of Detectives ate popcorn and listened to the Cubs and was unaware that the woman whose cage was a kitchen often dreamed of sharing his. Roger Dowling found he did not wholly deplore his old friend's obtuseness. The thought of searching for a new housekeeper was a disturbing one.

A Cub hit the ball and it rose like human hope, accompanied by the frenzied voice of Lou Boudreau, until, like so many hopes, after a looping trajectory it died in an opponent's glove.